Splatterpunk's Basement of Horror

(a charity anthology)

Edited by

Jack Bantry

Published by
Splatterpunk Zine

ISBN 9798862176315

For all the splatterpunks who have left us too early.

CONTENTS

ACKNOWLEDGMENTS

I'd like to thank all the contributors for letting me use their stories in this anthology; Denis Privezentsev, for the super artwork; and Mike Dickinson, for once again doing a great job with the cover design. None of this would be possible without all of your generosity. And most importantly, thanks to YOU, the reader, for buying this book.

Splatterpunk's Basement of Horror is a charity anthology, with all royalties going to Herriot Hospice Homecare, who help people living with terminal cancer.

Girls Dying in Lonely Places
Brendan Vidito

1

His breathing filled her head. A husky, guttural wheeze that rippled gooseflesh down her arms and legs. The man stood over a hundred feet away, half-hidden in the shadow of an awning, but it sounded as though he were right behind her. Close enough to kiss the nape of her neck. Was it an aural illusion, a case of sound echoing across the snow-encrusted streets? Danielle didn't want to hang around and find out. She hitched her satchel higher over her shoulder. Wrapped her arms around her midsection. And walked faster, boots crunching in the snow.

A thought occurred to her. She rummaged in her satchel, gripping the canister of pepper spray in a gloved hand. It filled her with talismanic comfort. She released it only after a moment of hesitation, and her fingers crawled through a jumble of miscellaneous junk. Crumpled receipts, an eye shadow pallet with the cover missing, a pack of gum, and her tangled earphones. Finally, she found her cellphone. The feel of it, its weight, made her feel more secure.

But calling for help would only work if the man were a run-of-the-mill creep. And that unnatural breathing seemed to rule out that possibility. *All those women, they never had the chance to call for help. Why would you be any different?* She severed the thought before it could go any further. *It can't be him. The odds would be astronomical. It. Can't. Be. Him.*

She made a show of removing the phone from her satchel. Lifting it to her ear, she pretended to answer a call. "Hello. Yeah, it's me. What up?" She nodded at some imaginary voice in her head, said, "Yeah, I'm close. I'll see you soon. I'm pretty much around the corner." Then, because she couldn't help herself: "You're cleaning your gun collection? Cool. Sounds dangerous. Yeah. Okay. You too. See you soon."

Danielle glanced over her shoulder again. The man had emerged from under the awning and was now walking, undeterred, in her direction. The shadows had peeled away from the lower half of his face, revealing a hideous rictus. Maybe it was a trick of the light, but his mouth appeared too wide for his head. Teeth crowded and filed to predatory points. Despite the distance that separated them, Danielle observed these details with magnified clarity. As though they flickered—hallucinatory—across her mind's eye. The wind cooled the sweat beading along her hairline. *It's can't be him. Please not him.* She snapped her gaze back to the sidewalk ahead and doubled her already rapid pace, lungs forming urgent patterns in the air.

Okay. You're going to jump into the first cab you see. If it doesn't stop, throw yourself in front of the fucking thing. She scanned the street. Empty. How could that be? She'd spent more time at her friend Margie's than she'd planned. But still, it was only eight-thirty. There should be at least a few pedestrians or vehicles around despite the frigid weather.

She rounded the corner, moving downhill toward a closed liquor store. The parking lot was empty, and the shelves behind the dirty panes of glass smothered in shadow. Danielle stared at the inside of the shop as she passed, willing in vain for it to come to life. Lights flickering on, customers materializing in front of colorful displays. But, of course, it remained dark and unmoving. Her eyes darted in their sockets, scanning the street once more for any signs of escape. Again, she perceived nothing but cold desolation.

The breathing increased in volume, and beneath it, Danielle recognized the crunch of boots on hard snow. The footfalls timed to fill the brief silence between her hastening steps. She groaned. Her stomach knotted and turned.

The reflection in the liquor store window revealed the man had nearly closed to the gap between them. He was much taller than he looked from a distance—six and a half feet or more, towering above her reflection like something out of a nightmare. Danielle knew if she ran now, he would chase her, and the tension building inside her chest would erupt into full-blown panic. Her short, slightly overweight frame wouldn't stand a chance. The man wasn't muscular— quite the opposite. But his gloved hands appeared to be in possession of an extra joint. Or was that an illusion: a warped reflection on dirty glass? Whatever the case, she needed to do something quick. Otherwise, the man would continue to hold the advantage.

Before she could think her actions through. Before she could stop herself. Danielle turned around—fists balled into mallets—and screamed, "FUCK OFF!"

The man stopped dead several paces in front of her, his huge, deformed hands hanging at his sides. They were no illusion. An icy wind blew, stirring a fine mist of snow that sparkled under the streetlamps. A car horn blared in the distance. It sounded miles away.

Danielle opened her mouth, closed it again. Adrenaline surged, heightening her senses. Cold sweat trickled down her back. She stared into the man's face. At first, she failed to make sense of his features. They looked hazy, smeared across the surface of his skull. Then she realized he was wearing a mask. Or, rather, dark pantyhose that distorted the features underneath. There was the hint of an upturned nose. Wide, unblinking, black eyes. Oily hair plastered to a pale forehead. His mouth was the only feature that wasn't distorted. A ragged tear in the pantyhose exposed his wide toothy grin.

Danielle gagged on her terror and took an instinctive step back. *Jesus fuck. What is that thing?* His smile stretched to further obscene proportions. A thread of tobacco-stained saliva oozed out between his teeth and dribbled onto his chest. He held out one of his monstrous hands, the fingers splayed, and strode toward her. She opened her mouth to scream, but the sound lodged in her throat. She was going to die here. Alone. No memories flashed through her mind. No highlight reel of her fleeting existence. There was nothing but the cold and the man's grinning face filling her vision.

Blood thundered in her ears. The ground began to shake. *I don't want to die. Please.* She smelled him now, a mixture of stale semen and blood. His fingers grazed her throat. She could feel the jagged nails under his gloves. The hum of an engine filled the air. She took another step back. Her heel caught on a patch of ice and she began to fall. Twin headlights pinned her. A bus roared around the corner. Lights spilling from its windows like a miracle.

Her ass struck the sidewalk with such force an involuntary howl escaped her lips. The man stood above her, eclipsing the almost full moon with his masked head. On all fours, Danielle lunged into the road—heedless of danger—springing in front of the bus in time to hear the screaming hiss of the brakes. Every muscle in her body tensed. She prepared herself for impact, for pain. But the bumper only nudged her shoulder. Mouth dry, she scrambled to her feet and ran to the door, slammed her fists against the Plexiglas panes.

"Open the door. Open the door."

The doors hissed open. The driver was pale and wild eyed.

10

"What the fuck is wrong with you?" he demanded.

She glanced behind her in time to see the man slinking into the shadows beside the liquor store. Once he was half-submerged in darkness, he pointed one long finger in her direction and smiled. Her bowels turned to water, her knees to rubber.

Doe-legged, she climbed into the bus. The driver watched her, breathing hard.

"What bus is this?"

He told her.

"That won't take me home," Danielle said. She sounded years younger, a frightened child.

"Do you still want a ride?"

"Please."

She fumbled in her pockets for change. Found a few pieces and tried, with trembling fingers, to drop them into the coin slot. One clattered against the floor, another got stuck on the edge of the slot and refused to move any further. The driver held out a placating hand.

"It's okay," he said.

He seemed to have calmed down, his agitation replaced by something like sadness. He pressed a button on the coin slot machine and a transfer ticket whirred into view. The driver pulled it free with thumb and forefinger and extended it to Danielle. She took it, her movements slow. Hugging her arms around her chest, she moved to the back of the bus—it was empty—and dropped into one of the plastic seats. She trembled so hard her teeth chattered. Tears had gathered in her eyes but refused to fall, turning the interior of the bus into a blurry, impressionistic smear. She looked at her hands, awash in sickly blue fluorescent light, and watched them shake as the bus droned along its route.

Seconds or minutes later—she couldn't tell, shock had dulled her perception of time—her cellphone buzzed. She dug it out of her satchel, desperate for familiarity. The screen glowed with a message from Wesley. *C'mon, not now.* She'd dumped him yesterday, and he had been texting her nonstop ever since. Begging her to take him back. Apologizing for not being a better boyfriend. Blaming her for ruining his life. It was pathetic and only made her feel better about leaving him. She was tired of feeling like shit, like she could never do anything right.

Without reading the block of text he'd sent her, Danielle typed *NOT NOW* and stabbed the send button. She dropped the phone back into her satchel and leaned her head back. Took a deep breath. Tried to steady her heart rate. Her ringtone blared, making her jump. She snatched her phone again and answered. "What do you want?"

Silence. She waited, her brows rising with impatience. A mouth clicked on the other end of the line. "You're going to regret leaving me." The voice was strained, choked with tears, but still recognizable as Wesley.

"Wesley, what are you—"

The phone beeped and went silent. She moved it away from her face. Frowned at the words CALL ENDED blinking across the screen. It came to her in a rush of intuition. Were Wesley's threat and the appearance of the masked man somehow connected? On the heels of that thought, she remembered something Margie had told her that evening: "One thing the news seems to leave out is the fact that most of the victims had a jealous or angry man in their lives. An envious coworker, a rejected lover, or a pissed off ex-boyfriend. That can't be a coincidence."

"No," Danielle whispered to the pale reflection on the bus window. "It can't."

Danielle didn't know how long she was on the bus. But eventually, it pulled into the station and released her back into the cold. Not missing a beat, she boarded the right bus and ended up down the street from the duplex she rented. A few hurried steps brought her to the front door. She dug her keys from her satchel. Clumsily slid them into the lock.

And pushed her way inside, immediately closing the door and locking the deadbolt behind her.

With her back against the door, she closed her eyes and took a deep draught of air. A wave of nausea passed through her stomach as her adrenaline waned. All she wanted to do was curl up on the couch with a kitchen knife and let her tears flow.

She took a step toward the closet, intending to stow her coat, when her boot scraped against something on the floor. Bending down, she picked up a pair of black leather gloves. They stank of tobacco, sweat, and blood. Crude stitching connected strips of leather to accommodate extra finger joints.

Danielle inhaled a trembling breath. The man she'd evaded in the street was no run-of-the-mill creep. She'd always known this, even without the confirmation of the gloves clutched in her hand. But the self-preserving part of her brain had tried to shrink away from the truth. It was, after all, too horrifying to contemplate. *You'll regret leaving me.* Wesley's words ricocheted inside her skull. The man. He'd be back tonight—there was no doubt of that. And she had to be ready. She had no other choice, because the alternative was death.

2

Danielle sat alone on Margie's couch and sipped red wine. Music drifted from the record player. The radiator under the window clicked and gurgled. While she waited for Margie to return from the kitchen, Danielle pulled her phone from her satchel and glanced at the screen. She regretted it right away. Thirty-two unread messages from Wesley, the latest delivered only seconds ago. It said: PLEASE DON'T DO THIS TO ME. As she stared, another message appeared: DUCKING BITCH. She frowned, squeezed the power button, and put her phone away. At that moment, Margie returned with a plate of cheese and crackers in one hand and a wineglass in the other. She set the plate on the coffee table and dropped onto the couch, almost spilling her wine.

"You didn't need to do that," Danielle said, gesturing to the plate.

"Nothing heals a broken heart like cheese."

"I appreciate it, but I'm fine. It was my decision. Wesley had it coming."

Margie made a sound of agreement. "I'm glad you dumped his skinny ass. He's a fucking asshole."

"I'm glad I have your support," Danielle said and extended her wine glass.

"Always, babe."

They clinked glasses.

Margie downed the rest of her wine and leaned over to pinch a cube of cheese from the plate. "What do you think the asshole is up to now, anyway? You dumped him, what, like five minutes before coming here?"

"Pretty much." Danielle had another sip of wine. Let it roll around her mouth before going on. "He took it hard. Cried. Probably still is. I don't know."

"Oh yeah, he's still crying," Margie said and uttered one of her infrequent rusty laughs. But it died on her lips after a few seconds. Her expression grew serious. Danielle could almost see a new thought enter her mind. "But, seriously, as your friend, I feel like I have to warn you. Guys like Wesley tend to *overreact*. Their anger and resentment after a breakup can spiral out of control. For the next few days, be careful, okay?"

Danielle placed her wine on the coffee table. "What do you mean?"

"You've been keeping up with the news, right?"

"Of course."

She was talking about the recent surge in missing and murdered women across the city. Most of the bodies had been recovered in remote or unusual locations. Like that college student disemboweled at the bottom of an elevator shaft. Some women were even abducted from inside their homes—the doors and windows still locked. And it seemed to be the work of one man. A serial killer—masked and deformed—spotted many times on grainy CCTV footage. But most unsettling of all, this phenomenon seemed to be happening everywhere. Not just in the city…but all over the country. And, some believed, around the world.

"What does that have to do with Wesley?" Danielle said.

Margie sat up. Contemplated her empty wineglass for a beat. And looked Danielle full in the face. "Alright, I'm going to tell you something, but promise me you won't think I'm crazy." When Danielle nodded, Margie heaved a deep breath, said, "There's a theory going around online—I know, I know—that the man responsible for the murders is some kind of manifestation of male rage." She struggled to find the right words. "Like a tulpa, a thought form."

"I don't follow."

"It's hard to explain, but in a way, it's a being made from someone's thoughts. It has its own agency and intelligence. Like if your imaginary friend suddenly came to life."

"But it's not real. It's myth, folklore."

"Who the fuck knows?" said Margie. "A lot of people seem to believe tulpas are real. Case in point, there's group of guys online—probably mean, ugly virgins—who've been trying to bring one into existence for years. They have a website. Hold on."

She grabbed her phone from the coffee table, tapped the screen a few times, and handed it to Danielle. The site was ugly and amateurish. It consisted of two pages. A poorly written manifesto fueled by hatred and misogyny. And as a forum where men wrote vile messages about women and discussed their attempts to create a tulpa. As Danielle scrolled through the forums—frowning and shaking her head—one word kept coming up: Mensch.

She asked Margie for clarification.

"These assholes pick up one philosophy book and think they're cultured," said Margie. "It's a play on Nietzsche's concept of the Übermensch, the superior man of the future. The dick cheese squad use it as the name for their hypothetical tulpa."

"Jesus Christ."

"Right?" Margie took her phone back and placed it out of reach on the coffee table. "So yeah, what if these guys somehow managed to create something deadly? I know it sounds crazy, but what's going on in the world right now doesn't make much sense either." She threw a quick, bewildered glance around the room. "I need more fucking wine." Margie strode to the kitchen and returned with the bottle. "One thing the news seems to leave out—" she said pouring them both a generous glass "—is the fact that most of the victims had a jealous or angry man in their lives. An envious coworker, a rejected lover, or—" her voice dropped several octaves "—a pissed off ex-boyfriend. That can't be a coincidence. I know this because the friends and family of the victims shared their stories online. And these men I'm talking about were rarely considered suspects. They all had watertight alibis. Are you with me so far?"

"Uh, yeah," Danielle said, trying to keep up with the flood of information.

"Okay, good. Because this is where it gets real crazy," Margie said. "What if this thing—the Mensch—can somehow be called, or summoned, or whatever, by one these angry dudes. They could be doing it on purpose or by accident. What I mean to say is, according to the theory, the Mensch is drawn, or willed into being somehow, by a man's negative emotions toward a specific woman. That's how it determines its victims. It feeds on all that rage, hatred, and passion. And like some patron saint of assholes, takes vengeance on innocent women."

"But it's not real. It can't be."

"Maybe not." Margie fell silent, grasped Danielle's hand. "But even if it's bullshit, that doesn't discredit the fact that a bunch of guys are getting together online to hate on women. It's important we protect ourselves. That's why I'm telling you this. Considering what just happened with Wesley, it would be shitty of me not to tell you what I know."

Danielle had known Margie since grade school. She was pragmatic, coldly rational. Believing in the supernatural was out of character, and for that reason Danielle was compelled to believe her. She saw the fear in her habitually hard eyes, noted the slight tremor in her voice. And that dread in turn infected her mind and spread throughout her body.

She blinked rapidly, set her mouth in a hard line. "I don't think you have to worry about Wesley. He might be an asshole, but he's not capable of hurting me. Intentionally or otherwise."

Wesley rocked back and forth on his mattress, clutching his stomach and sobbing. He was exhausted, his throat raw and sore. He didn't know how long he'd been crying in the dark. It could have been minutes. It could have been hours. Lost in his grief, time had no meaning anymore. He was adrift on a sea of pain and misery.

"Why would you leave me?" he whimpered. "I've been so good to you."

He looked up, eyes wet and swollen. On the bedside table sat a framed photograph of him and Danielle. He had an arm around her shoulder, and they were grinning for the camera. The barest hint of a smile touched his lips. Then his anger reared its head, as it often did when his sadness became too much to handle. It was blistering hot and blinding. His blood turned to molten metal. His cheeks burned. And his teeth clamped together. He seized the photograph and hurled it against the wall. The frame snapped and the glass shattered, raining shards over the dirty clothes and used dishes scattered across the floor. Someone in the apartment below banged against the ceiling and yelled for him to shut the fuck up, which only made him angrier.

He lunged across the room, slid the photograph— now liberated from its frame—to a bare spot on the floor. And stabbed Danielle's face with a jagged piece of glass. It dug into his palm, drawing blood, but his rage dulled the pain.

"Fuck you, you fucking bitch," he screamed, tears and spittle flying from his face.

The glass tore ragged white lines across Danielle's image. Piercing the paper and gouging the hardwood floor underneath.

"I hope you die, you selfish cunt!"

His anger grew and grew. An inferno fed an endless torrent of gasoline. It consumed everything inside him, enveloping old memories—not only of Danielle, but previous exes, his sister, and overbearing mother—and turned them into fuel. The rage soon become so overpowering it coalesced into an unspoken prayer. A supplication that shone outward like a beacon...

He sensed a presence in the room. A movement of the air. A subtle variation in the light. The sound of a floorboard creaking. A shadow fell over him, obscuring the photo, which was maimed and dotted with his blood. He rolled over into a sitting position.

A man towered above Wesley, his deformed hands dragging against the floor. He grinned, all pointed teeth and drooling tobacco-stained saliva. He wore black. And a crusty pair of pantyhose pulled over his head. Wesley stared, unable to move or speak. But he experienced no fear. Rather, he felt a kinship, a connection, with this man. He was a friend. He came to men in need, to punish selfish, cold bitches like Danielle.

The man hunched over and held out one of his monstrous hands, palm up. Knowing what he wanted—like he could see inside his head—Wesley held out the ruined photograph. Blood streaked down his arm and dripped from his elbow. The man accepted the offering with a modest bow. His watery black eyes crawled across the vandalized remains of Danielle's face. He opened his mouth in a smile somehow wider than before. Both his tongue and hard palate lined with crooked teeth.

"Give her what she deserves," Wesley said.

He squeezed his fist so hard blood spurted up between his fingers.

3

Danielle relaxed her fingers and let the gloves slap to the floor. She shrugged out of her coat and walked toward the basement stairs, switching lights on along the way. With each brisk step, she glanced over her shoulders, scanning the rooms of her rental duplex.

Silence. No sign of an intruder. The kitchen was the last place she checked on the main floor. Drawing a knife from the block, Danielle made her way downstairs. Holding the knife, she sidestepped around the space, making sure to never have her back to a doorway as she inspected every room. Bathroom. Office. Laundry alcove. Empty. Danielle allowed herself a small sigh of relief, knowing the night was far from over. The man would no doubt return. She would have to make the necessary preparations, meet the bastard on even ground.

In the laundry alcove, she stood with her back to the machines and opened the gun case against the wall. She placed her knife on top of the case and selected her shotgun. It was a gift from her father. He owned a hunt camp and she often spent time there with him, hunting partridge and deer. She broke open the weapon and slid two shells into the breech. Slipped a few more into her pocket as insurance. She closed the breech with a quick snap of her wrist.

A crash upstairs almost made her drop the gun.

"You didn't waste any time," she said.

Her fear had all but disappeared. She was nervous, wary, but the near-crippling terror she experienced earlier had subsided. Knowing Wesley was likely behind the appearance of the man emboldened her somewhat. His anger and resentment were things she could understand. As opposed to the elusive nature of her stalker. She lifted the recoil pad of the shotgun against her shoulder and took the basement stairs, one step at a time. The house was silent except for the faint hum of the water heater.

In the living room, she discovered the source of the disturbance. The lamp near the entrance lay broken on the floor. And behind it, hunched over and clad in black, was the man. Danielle gasped and took aim. The man lifted his head, now bare of its mask, and screamed, "Holy fuck. Don't shoot."

The voice was familiar. Danielle lowered her weapon.

"Margie?" she said. "What are you doing here? You scared the shit out of me."

"I felt like an asshole watching you leave my place after all the shit I told you. Didn't want you to spend the night alone." She straightened and held up a key. "I used the key you made me a couple years back to get inside. And I'm sorry about your lamp. I'm a clumsy bitch."

Danielle released a gust of breath. "It's fine. You're lucky I didn't blow your head off."

"Yeah, no shit. Why are you walking around with a shotgun?"

"You were right to be worried," Danielle said. "I saw the man from the news. He tried following me home."

Margie grabbed fistfuls of her hair. "Are you fucking kidding me?"

"What happens now?"

"How would I know?"

"What do you mean? You know more about this than I do."

20

"I'm just reading shit on the Internet."

Danielle laughed despite the situation. "Lock the door behind you. We need to be ready if he decides to show up."

Margie followed the instruction. She glanced outside to make sure the street was empty, her breath fogging the glass. Turned to face Danielle again. "Do you have a plan?"

"Let's have a look around the house, gather anything we can use as a weapon."

"We're not splitting up."

"Obviously."

Their first stop was the kitchen. Margie pulled the largest knife from the block and slipped it through one of her belt loops. For good measure, she reached for the meat tenderizer in the sink and tested its weight. Pleased, she held it at her side in a firm grip.

Afterwards, they proceeded to the basement. Danielle led the way, holding the shotgun like her father had taught her, sighing down the barrel. They appeared to be alone. Together, they entered the laundry room. Danielle crouched. Dragged the toolbox from under the stairs. Removed a box cutter and extended its blade. It was still sharp. Satisfied, she retracted the blade and slid the tool into her back pocket.

"We're as ready as we're ever going to be," she said.

Danielle looked over her shoulder at Margie, but her friend was gone, so was the basement. Behind her stretched an endless corridor. Pipes and cables, rusted or frayed, veined the ceiling. Its floor and walls covered in small, square tiles, like the kind found in a locker room shower. Blood and bits of human tissue stood out against the stark white ceramic. And the air reeked of spoiled meat.

Danielle scrambled to her feet, slid on the tile, and slapped a hand on the wall for support. *What the fuck is going on?* Something brushed against her foot. She kicked out in a violent frenzy. The object sailed further down the hall—a bra, faded blue and crusted with blood. A rusty wire pierced the fabric and stuck out at a jaunty angle. And then it hit her. Everywhere she looked: similar articles of clothing. Underwear. Dresses. Miniskirts. Pantyhose. Everything shredded and stained a dark, brownish red.

Did these belong to the missing and murdered women? How did I end up here? Her questions were interrupted by heavy footfalls beating the tile behind her. Before she could twist around, hot, rancid breath surged against the back of her neck. With a cry, Danielle turned, but only made it halfway before arms wrapped around her chest and squeezed. She discharged the shotgun, blowing a fist-sized hole in the wall.

She struggled, but the man pressed his knee into her spine and jerked her head back by the hair. Her lungs screamed for oxygen. Her head swam, her vision blurred. *Please. It can't end this way.* The shotgun slid from her grasp and clattered on the floor. As her consciousness ebbed, she remembered the box cutter. A flicker of hope surged through her as she reached around, squeezing her hand between her lower back and the man's chest. Her fingers managed to slip into her back pocket, brushing the plastic casing of the knife. *So fucking close.*

The man uttered a wheezing chuckle, like he knew what she was planning. With his mouth against her ear, he said, "Why would you leave me? I've been so good to you." The voice belonged Wesley, though distorted, husky, and choked with phlegm.

Danielle went rigid. An overwhelming feeling of disgust penetrated to the very center of her being. Then came the anger. *Wesley, that piece of shit. He gaslighted me for months. I almost believed I was the cause of all his problems. And now* he's *angry enough to want* me *dead? Fuck him. I'm the only one who has the right to be pissed.* Her fingers curled around the box cutter. She extracted the blade and plunged into toward the man's crotch. He howled and released his grip on Danielle. She plummeted to the floor, landing on her knees. Not wasting a second, she sprang up, filled her lungs, stumbled, recovered, and grabbed the shotgun. She twisted her body around, aimed, and fired. The man's chest blossomed into a vibrant corona of blood. With the box cutter sticking out of his crotch—wobbling from his movements—the man staggered backward and collapsed against the wall.

Danielle blinked and was back in her basement again. The shotgun was still in her grasp. She struggled to her feet, but a wave of dizziness overcame her, and she sank back down to the floor. Margie gaped in her direction, arms hanging at her sides.

"What the fuck happened? You disappeared. Why are you covered in blood?"

Danielle raised a hand to touch her face. Her fingers came away red and sticky.

"I saw the man. He tried to—"

She couldn't finish. The man stood behind Margie, holding the bloody box cutter above his head. Her warning came too late. The man swatted Margie aside and lunged toward Danielle. His chest wound was catastrophic. Rib bones glistened like long teeth through a ragged, still-leaking crater. Despite the damage, though, he still moved with homicidal determination. The box cutter plunged into Danielle's shoulder, missing her heart by inches. The pain was so overwhelming she could do nothing but gasp. The man dragged the blade down—slicing through her flesh like a white-hot branding iron—and *that* tore a scream from her throat. Then the blade stopped. There was a thud, the sound of metal meeting flesh.

Danielle looked up. Margie was preparing to deliver a second blow with the meat tenderizer. The man caught her wrist mid-swing and broke her arm at the elbow with an effortless jerk. The bone stuck out of her forearm like a white stick in a pool of blood.

Margie howled. The tenderizer dropped from her grasp and clanged against the floor. Seething with impatience, the man recalled his attention to Danielle. But when he tried to continue his work with the box cutter, it was gone. In its place, a ragged wound glistened on her chest. The box cutter was in her hand. She raised it and stabbed the blade into his right eye. He threw his body back, his scream pounding against her eardrums.

Here was her chance. She dragged the shotgun across the floor. Broke it open. Dug two shells out of her pocket. Jammed them into the breach. Closed the weapon and took aim.

In her mind, it was no longer the man standing there—the Mensch—but Wesley. His face flushed from weeping and tears on his cheeks. He looked pathetic.

"I refuse to be your victim," Danielle said and squeezed the trigger.

The space between his shoulders exploded in a shower of blood and torn flesh. The Mensch dropped to his knees and slumped to one side, convulsing with agony. Margie rushed over, the large kitchen knife held in her good hand, and stabbed him in the stomach and neck. Blood spurted toward the ceiling in thick ropes. With a groan, Danielle got to her feet and pointed the shotgun at his face. Breathless, Margie stepped away to give her room.

"Wesley sent you here, didn't he?"

The Mensch said nothing, only moaned. Danelle sensed his fear, his shame. The exhilaration that flooded her body was unlike anything she'd previously experienced. She knew, looking into his face, what he was thinking—like she could see inside his head. His prey had never turned on him before. The rules had changed. His purpose, his reason for being, had been thrown into question. And it was time for Danielle to provide him with direction.

She lowered on one knee, pointed the barrel under his chin.

"You answered to Wesley's anger. Now you answer to mine." She leaned forward. The still-hot barrel caused the skin on the Mensch's chin to dimple. He squirmed, uncomfortable. "Go to his apartment. Tell him we're done ...for good. Do you understand?"

Through the pain, the Mensch's black eyes glistened with new purpose.

Danielle's anger had become a part of him. And to survive, he had no other choice but to do as she instructed. She had, after all, changed the rules…

Wesley paced his room, kneading the bandage around his hand. Blood showed through the cloth, and his palm still hurt from where the glass had cut him, but he didn't care. His mind was too busy going over the possibilities. Was the man killing Danielle at this very moment? Did her screams fill the cold darkness of the night? Was she suffering? Or did she die quickly? He hoped for the former. She deserved all the pain that man—his friend—could administer.

He imagined showing up at her funeral, her friends and family flocking to him with embraces and condolences. Tears ran down his cheeks as he thanked them. Then, glancing over at the closed casket, he said, "I wish I'd been there in her final moments."

Which, in a way, was true. Part of him wanted to see her die. Wanted to watch the blood drain from her body. The light fade from her eyes. Those final spasms as her nervous system rebelled against the inevitable. It would be the ultimate form of closure.

The lights dimmed, and he sensed a presence in the room. He turned. The man stood near the door, hunched over, and covered in blood. Wesley thrilled at the sight. The man must have brutalized Danielle. He was drenched in her lifeblood, and some pieces of her flesh and hair even clung to his clothes. But the longer he stared, the more he realized the blood came from the man's own body. Especially the wounds on his chest and groin. Wesley took a step back. His thrill evaporated. Replaced by disappointment, anger.

"Well, did you do it or not?" he demanded.

The man reached inside his pocket, removed something, and tossed it toward Wesley. It seesawed toward to the floor and landed next to his foot—the photograph of him and Danielle.

"Why are you giving this to me? Did you do your fucking job or not?"

His anger flared anew, but it was short lived. The man stomped toward him and wrapped deformed hands around his throat. Before Wesley knew it, his anger was stillborn, replaced by a soul-crushing, all-pervasive terror. He screamed, loud, long, and hard, but that too was cut short as the man plunged a hand into his stomach and yanked out a fistful of entrails. He choked on the blood rising into his throat. The man wrapped an intestine around his hand and pulled harder, freeing several more feet of Wesley's insides, until something snapped with a bright-white flash of agony. A geyser of blood erupted from his mouth and he dropped to the floor. As his vision faded to black, Wesley watched a thick pool of his own blood spread toward the photograph on the floor. He noticed Danielle's smile was still visible through the gashes he'd inflicted with the piece of glass. It wasn't a smile of joy or happiness: this was a smile of triumph.

Skins
Candace Nola

As her vision cleared, Cassandra looked around as if waking from a dream, finding herself in a nightmare. Blood dripped from the walls, from the ceiling, from her hands and face. Decimated corpses were strewn at her feet. Thick clumps of tissue, organs, and guts littered the floor everywhere she looked. A butcher's knife glistened at her feet. Scattered white bone gleamed beneath red gore. She stared at the mess, then at herself, running her hands over her skin, moulded to her body, tight and supple, glistening with crimson splatter. She dropped the objects in her hands and turned toward the door. No one was left to laugh at her as she vanished out the door and into the night. No one would laugh at her again. The anger consumed her. She never saw the figure enter the alley as she fled.

Fury drove her through her the alleys, beneath the railroad trestle, down to the docks toward the bridge beyond. Anger and humiliation cycled through her mind, again and again, the events played out in her head. The laughter as they ripped her mask off and tore her cloak from her body. Their shocked faces as they took in her full appearance, the scars that crisscrossed over her skin, the stitches that held her within. Rejected and cast out once again. *Why?* She had done everything right. She had become one of them. Re-invented herself for them, learned their ways, their lingo, their likes, their style. She had donned a whole new skin just for them.

Why didn't they want her? Wasn't she good enough for them? After all she had done. All her efforts to change who she was to show she was worthy of their acceptance? Why wasn't it enough? Why wasn't she enough? Why wasn't she wanted?

She stood by the railing, chest heaving, tears pouring down her face. Mascara and eyeliner creating black tears as she stared at the water churning fifty feet below. Frigid air swept messy blood-stained curls from her face and chilled her flesh as she stared at nothing, through the water, into oblivion. It was time. She knew it. Every essence of her being knew it. Her body vibrated with it, yearned for it, longed for the peace that would come, for the relief, the release.

Fear had fled her long ago, years, minutes, seconds, a moment ago. Her resolve steeled her spine. Hardened her eyes. Dried her tears, the last she would ever shed. Slowly, Cassandra straightened and shed her cloak for the last time. The night air swept over her skin, causing her flesh to bristle beneath the skin. She pulled the shears from her bag and began to snip at the translucent fishing line that held her together. She started at her neck, snipping the first stitch right at the hollow of her throat, then followed it around her jawline, to her temple and back down.

As she took a deep cleansing breath, she shook the skin free and began to snip the stitches that ran down her chest and torso and along her limbs. She cut through the ribbons, the leather, the laces she had used. All pretty things to hide the rotting seams. She barely flinched as she cut through the skin, piercing her, piece by piece. Pulling and ripping the thread free of her bones, releasing the flesh that clung to her own.

Minutes later, she stepped free of the flesh that bound her and let it drop in a heap on the pavement. She slid a hand over her head, brushing back the scalp that was no longer hers, the thick mane of curls that still dripped red droplets when she moved. She let it fall to the ground and set her own hair free. Limp, straight, and raven black, her hair fell down her back, kissing her tailbone as it settled into place for the first time in months.

She moved, naked and free, gripped the rail, lifted one leg, pulled, lifted the other leg. The water rushed by, roiling with white-capped waves, ripples crashing on the rocks that flanked the sides. It called to her, over and over, her name on the wind, whispers in her ears, screaming in her mind. A singular rage, one command, one final need to meet. It would be so simple. She gazed into the night, one hand clutching the steel beam to her right, her feet balanced on the precipice. Her heart was already dead and broken, her soul flickering, having spent its last flame. She had nothing left.

A shudder ran through her. She inhaled deeply, letting it out slowly. A shout rang out, followed by pounding footsteps. She turned her head, curious but already letting go. No one would stop her. Nothing would save her, could save her. Their eyes met. Time slowed. Her eyes widened. The man froze. It was him.

Looking for her? Hoping to save her? Rescue her? Maybe scar her broken mind further? Lie to her again?

Rage and bitterness gripped her as she floated toward the abyss. Nothing mattered, not anymore. She fell. The water beneath her seemed to stand still. The ripples and waves barely made a sound. She fell to her death while he watched from above. Her lifetime connecting them both one instant at a time. Tears clung to his cheeks while hate dried them from hers. Second by second, her life rewound itself through her mind, and his. Together they blinked, an image shifted, and blazed in their brain.

A baby, discarded and unwanted, followed by years of sadness, of being an outcast, a half-breed, a forgotten, invisible thing. An object to be used and tolerated, not loved, or adored, not protected, not cared for. Humiliation, fear, and cruelty at the hands of her classmates. At the cruel hands of men, driven by hate and lust.

He blinked.

Her first attack. Black night, pain and blood, rage, and helplessness. Assaulted. Violated. Beaten. Left on the floor. She was seven.

She blinked. White noise roared in her ears.

The first group assault, first one of many. Pain, savage pain in her body. Objects in places they did not belong. Fists punch, beat her, hold her down as they each take their turn. Blood runs freely as they mount her, use her, torture her, and laugh. One pissed on her like garbage, kicked her a final time, then left her in ruins on a basement floor. Tears flow. Rage builds. She was ten.

He blinked tears away, remembering how she screamed in the night. Her nightmares forcing her to relive this and more, every night, every day. Stealing her joy, crippling her life, altering her mind. Trauma lived within her, reminding her daily of the nothing she would always be.

He saw her at fourteen. Heartbroken and lonely. Friendless, haunted, tortured and scorned. He saw the years of pain and abuse. He saw the birthday parties that no one came to. He saw the tears she shed at night. Saw the pain she kept locked inside as she walked through the school hallways, alone and rejected. He saw the first verse, penned and stained by her tears. He saw her journals full of heartache and fear.

He saw her don the first mask, an awful Halloween thing. Her dark eyes glittered within; her lips curled up ever so slightly as she looked in the mirror. It hid her pain, her bruises, her shame. She slipped into a cloak, black as midnight, and looked again at her reflection, another small smile beneath the mask. She could be new. Someone different. He heard her thoughts as if they were his own.

Actors did it every day, didn't they? Just slip on a mask, a costume, a new voice. Become something new, someone new. She could play a role, couldn't she? If it stopped the pain, she could. She would.

She blinked, and she remembered the second mask. Simple silicone, smooth and black, wide eyes like a baby doll, a painted-on smile that hid her frown. The schoolgirl uniform with long white socks, the preppy girl look, the backpack full of books. Glass with thin frames completed her look. She entered the school, another new place, hopeful for this persona to blend, for the new mask to work. She saw their stares, remembered their jeers.

What are you, some kind of freak? Why can't you be normal? Why can't you fit in? Why are you hiding your face? Are you disfigured or scarred? What a loser, a freak, a skank, a wannabe goth, a clown, a joker.

The names went on and on, every day, every hour. No matter what she tried, she was cast out and rejected. The preppies, the goths, the skaters, the jocks. The mean girls, the dancers, the hippies, the stoners, Hell, she was too much of an outcast for the other outcasts. She wandered the hallways, invisible and shattered, wondering why any of it mattered. But it did. She just wanted to belong, somewhere, anywhere, to anyone that would have her. God, she only wanted to breathe, to be seen.

She inhaled and breathed, a tear slipping free, here in these moments, she still felt the pain. Her loneliness, the shame, her constant despair. She blinked, and she saw him witnessing this. He watched, breath caught in his chest, as she continued to fall. He blinked, and he saw her, one memory more.

She was eighteen and needed something new. On her own, alone in the world, free to do as she pleased. She could be anyone now, not just the weird girl with the too dark eyes, bad attitude, and velvet black cape. She saw the new suit, a tight-fitting corset, black leather, and ribbon. A masquerade mask that hid the pain in her eyes, hid the scar at her temple, and along her cheekbone. Hid her broken parts and quiet shame.

She felt her lips curl as she slid the leather on. Tight like a new skin, it hugged every curve, every limb, smooth and silky inside. She swept her hair back, tied it up in a braid. The raven on her shoulder flexed as she turned, admiring her new self in the mirror. She wore it home that day, tried out a new voice. Re-invented once more, she rejoined the world, hoping the new her would be accepted this time.

He blinked, and he saw how that ended. A bad night in a bar, fake friends left her alone. A strange man with pretty words. A spiked drink and a lonely, naïve girl. It ended badly with her bloody once more, discarded in a dumpster, nude, scarred, stabbed multiple times. She bled and waited to die. He cried.

She blinked.

He reached the railing, her name on his lips. He saw her blink. He did the same, tears escaping down his cheeks as a new image consumed him. The first time he saw what she had done for him, because of the words he had uttered. Words that hurt her like none ever had. Words that made her feel more unworthy and ashamed of her hidden pain. Words that caused her to change.

That night she came to him, to his hotel suite, wearing a new outfit. The same his new girlfriend had on that day. The same tight fit, the same color shirt, designer heels and bag to match. Even her hair had been carefully colored and styled to match the woman that slept beside him.

"Isn't this better?" she asked him, twirling around. "See, I can be her. I can be anyone you need." She giggled and batted her eyes, eerily similar to the woman in his bed. Her voice, her accent, her manners were all the same. She must have been following her for months to perfect her persona so well. His heart crumpled as she put on her act for him, begged him to come back, all while his new girlfriend slept off her drunken stupor from their engagement party that evening.

"Cassie, stop." He rose from the bed, keeping his voice quiet. He went over to her, seeing the madness in her heavily made-up eyes. It chilled him to the bone. Clammy cold sweat trickled down his spine as he gently guided her from the room.

"Stop what?" She demanded. "Isn't this what you wanted?" Anger filled her eyes, but her tone remained that of his girlfriend, sweet and melodic.

"You said I wasn't enough. That I couldn't be what you wanted. Isn't this what you want? If she is what you want, then this should be good enough, too."

"That's not what I meant, and you know it." He said, still guiding her toward the door. "I need you to understand that. You are not her. You are still you. We just do not match. You are not what I want, not what I thought I wanted, not anymore. Don't you see that?"

"But I did this for you, don't you see that? All the things I did, I did for you. I'm pretty now. I lost weight. I changed my hair, my style, my voice. I learned to be her. Isn't that what you wanted? Isn't that enough?" Her voice became smaller, breaking on the last word, like a child on the verge of tears.

He opened the door, walking her through it. "You can't just become someone else. That's not how it works. You can't be what she is. You will never be what she is. You will never be enough. You were never enough. Please leave before I have to call the police."

"I'm still not good enough...?" She said again quietly, a question but meant more for her than for him. He shut the door and watched through the peephole as she finally cried. Tears streaking the carefully applied mask of make-up. He stood there watching as she fell apart, alone in the hotel hallway, before she silently walked away.

He blinked the tears away as he realized that was the moment that broke her. After everything she had endured, he had been the one to break her completely and irrevocably. He watched the waters churn beneath her. Watched the wind ripple her hair, billowing it out around her like a dark halo. He saw her eyes, frozen on his, black and sparkling, gleaming with rage, with hurt, with pain. He saw her, finally, as she should have been, not for what she became.

She blinked; the scene changed.

She stood in her basement, in a puddle of blood and gore. Her body was nude, gleaming in the fluorescent light as she slipped on the new skin. This one fit just right, tight like the leather she used to favor, sleek and warm. She carefully began to guide the fishing line thread into the flesh, stitching herself inside. She had removed the bones one at a time, after the blood and organs were discarded like trash. She rinsed it carefully on the steel table where she did her best work. Zippers and scissors and thread of all kinds littered the bench beside her, with the chemicals she needed to keep the skin soft and fresh. They didn't last very long, but she liked this one the best.

She shifted slightly, adjusting her toes, feeling them squelch inside the new skin, inside the new slick sheaths that were now her own. She giggled as they wriggled inside the moist flesh and continued to sew. Her hands were steady from practice. People stared when she roamed the streets at night, but no one dared laugh as she practiced being her new self, adorned with stitches and zippers and tight-fitting clothes. New body, new hair, new colored eyes, a whole new mask that was more than a disguise.

She was becoming something better with each new suit, every new persona. She had perfected her laughs, different types of voice. Her masks hid her scars. The perfect flesh of each skin hid what had been done to her. She only wanted to fit in, to be someone comfortable in her own skin. She was discovering how, even if it was new skin, it was still her skin, wasn't it? She created it, freed it, zipped it, and sewed it.

She became a new, better version of herself. Or rather, society's vision of better, of accepted, of fair skinned and right. *His* vision of what she should be. She only wanted to fit in, to belong somewhere at last. She just wanted to exhale, to breathe, safe and free, wanted and welcomed.

One of the new suits would surely be the key to freeing the sobs she kept locked in her chest.

She blinked. Teardrops fell free from her eyes. She saw herself, a monster, the thing she had become. He blinked, staggering from the scene that lit up his mind.

Cassie stood silent in the pitch-black night of October. Cloaked in her velvet, the dagger strapped to her side. Her new skin was waiting, almost in stride. She watched like a panther, waiting for the woman to jog by. Her feet pounded on the pavement. The moonlight shone from above, lighting the trail along the lakeside. The woman was perfect, beautiful, and fit. Long hair, sun-kissed skin, shaped like a goddess, with a bright personality to match.

Cassie had been watching her for weeks, as the skin she now wore became decayed and weak. It was graying, rotting, wearing thin in places. Cassie had resisted as long as she was able, but it was time for a new mask, a new way of life. The woman was smart, had a good job at home. Cassie had noticed she lived alone and rarely met with friends. No one would notice a slight change in her routine, a small adjustment while Cassie took over, transitioned to this new life, her new identity.

She closed her eyes, listening to the woman's steady breaths, her footsteps coming closer. She inhaled, held it, and drew her blade. A moment, a footstep, one footstep more. She lunged forward, a beast exploding from darkness, a flurry of rage. The woman made no sound as she fell, throat already gushing from the savage blow. Cassie caught her and pulled backwards, disappearing into the bushes, then fled into the night.

She blinked. Cassie saw the woman on her table, crimson staining the floor. Her pale skin covered in red, the slope of her breasts, her taut supple thighs, the flat of her stomach, and the curve of her hips. She carved her open, slicing through the skin, releasing fat, muscle, and bone from within. Cassie worked all night in her own rotting skin.

Carefully, she released the flesh from the wearer and set it aside.

She grabbed her needles and sat down to sew, making a new suit for herself, beautiful and free. The world would love her in this one. She would be everything good, as society decreed, all *He* had deemed worthy of love and acceptance. This one would make everything right. She would show them. They would all finally see.

She sewed all night as the rotting flesh she sat in oozed from her body. Strips of decaying tissue shed from her in slimy bits of gore. Patches of grey slid from her arms, her legs, her face as she sewed. She shrugged them away, not bothered at all. The new suit would be ready soon. She let the old one fall, covered in sweat and blood, rot and pus and bodily fluids. She sewed, smiling a grin so big it sloughed the skin from her cheeks, showing glimpses of her face hidden beneath.

Cassie stood when she finished, naked in her flesh. She refused to look in the mirror as she stepped into the perfectly finished skin suit. She had added more zippers to hide the stitches, black silk ribbons corseted the spine. Leather straps wrapped around each shin, adding detail to hide the joining of seams. She had cleaned it, scrubbed it, oiled it until it glowed. The tanning agent made it sparkle as if kissed by the sun. The mounds of the breasts were perky and plump, fitting snugly against her own, concealing her scarred flesh. More ribbons ran along each arm, hiding the stitch marks beneath satin, these wrapped her collarbone and connected at the base of the skull, an automatic choker to accent her neck.

She pulled the face up, and over her own, then finally turned to look in the mirror. It fit her like a glove, except around the eyes and mouth. A little sag there made her eyes droop like a sad clown, but an easy fix with needle and thread would tighten that up. She sat down to sew the face on her own. Her smallest needle made quick work of it all. Tiny pinches around each eye as she secured the new flesh.

Tiny dots of crimson circled her sockets as the needle punctured and pulled, but she barely felt it.

She was euphoric and content, settled within. The suit was beautiful, her best work to date. *She* was beautiful, she finally felt. This would be the one to set her path right. A good life, a house to move into, a job to assume. Friends to be made, love to find. Surely a man would adore this version of her. Surely, *He* would adore her. He had to love her now.

She looked in the mirror and fluffed up the hair. It fell to her shoulders in a chaos of waves, rumpled from the night's proceedings but still a gorgeous mane. Her dark eyes gleamed in the mirror; a smile lifted the plump lips. She ran her hands down the body, across her stomach and hips, the carefully sutured opening that led to her sex. The ribbons and leather that adorned the tanned flesh. It was perfect. She was perfect. She turned and plodded sleek manicured feet across the blood-soaked floor, not caring how the crimson had turned tacky and cold nor how the tissues clung to her toes.

She hummed to herself as she retrieved the hose. Turning the water on, she began to rinse the gore down the drain. As the water sluiced across the floor, she grabbed the broom and began to sweep the chunks of organs and brain tissue into a pan. She dumped them in the grinder, along with the bones, and set it to churn the remains into paste. As the machine clanked and whirred, she twirled across the pink swirling floor, dancing to music only she could hear. She lifted the hose and finished rinsing the room, spraying the walls and ceiling free from the dark splatter.

Finally finished, she hosed herself down, giggling with laughter. She was wet and thriving, a goddess freed from her chains. She padded from the room, seeking clothing for a night on the town. She was ready to be seen, accepted, worshipped, and adored. It was her time. She could feel it.

He blinked. Watched as the image faded. He knew how that one ended already. Another rejection, more humiliation. No one had been able to see past the stitches and the slightly discolored skin. Fear had soaked the room when she stepped inside. A slow murmur began to rise as they noticed how the face did not quite fit her eyes. How it sagged around her mouth and didn't quite attach properly to her nose. Tension had built the closer she came, and then someone had called her a freak, a misfit, a badly costumed joke. They knew something was wrong with the skin she was in, an old movie prop, a decaying silicone wrap, something was wrong, but they dared not say what. It did not matter, as the names were enough. Their rejection, their laughter, their stares, and their jeers triggered the fury Cassie carried within. She blinked away tears and their slaughter began.

His stomach churned like the waters below. He clutched the railing, unable to speak. Cassie kept falling, her eyes locked on his. He had been too late to save her from this. A single tear fell from his eyes as he watched the heartbroken girl drop to the sea. Her body sheathed in the moonlight. Her face was now gentle with the peace that would soon come. Her hair billowed around her; a midnight halo fit for the fallen angel she would become.

She blinked. Her eyes glistened with wetness, but tears did not fall. She watched him, loved him, loathed him, one and the same. The final cause of the breaking from pain.

He blinked, and the image changed. One more memory filled her mind.

A montage of murders, her stealing their skin, months of watching and planning and trying to fit in. As she fled each scene, vanishing with her prey, a shadow of a figure entered each frame. Just a second too late to catch her, a minute too slow to stop her. A man approached each scene, taking in the violence, the gore, the telltale splatter. She saw his head shake, his lips silently move, then watched as he cleaned up the remains, the evidence, and clues. She watched as he cried, all the while trying to protect her from the penance to come.

She was sloppy, a rookie, a phoenix feeding on rage. The police would have found her, if not for his help. He had done this, knowing her pain was somewhat his fault. He did not know how to help her, but could not turn her in. Instead, he followed her, and cleaned as she killed, destroying all sight of any blood being spilled. Her pain consumed him, became his burden to bear. Society had failed her, again and again. Kindness was such a small thing, but had never been shown. He had loved her once, but then had turned cruel. He did not understand her, the depths of her rage, her need to be loved, to be accepted by him, by anyone.

She blinked. A small smile lifted her lips. He blinked. He saw her. Understanding blossomed on her face. For once, he saw her, as he should have all along. He accepted. He loved her; he mourned her as she vanished. She blinked and was gone, sunk into the abyss. The ocean embraced her, kissed her cold flesh. Took her as she was, empty, broken and shattered. She was free, accepted, and finally enough. In the final second, that was all that mattered.

Jeff Strand & Bridgett Nelson
Mac & Millie

Mac

I'd looked at a shocking number of dicks for a guy who was almost entirely heterosexual.

I mean pictures, of course. I didn't have men lined up in my apartment. What I needed was the perfect dick pic for the dating site I was using. It had to be large, of course, but not so large that a potential recipient would say, "Oh, no, goodness no, I could never accommodate that!" As straight as possible—no weird curves. Circumcised, obviously.

Finally, I found it. Yes, this would be the penis I presented to the ladies on the site!

And then I realized I was going about this all wrong.

I might as well come out and say it: I was using this site to find a murder victim. My brain is a little mixed-up, and I have this uncontrollable desire to take human lives. Okay, *female* lives. I swear I'm not a misogynist. Don't read anything into the fact that all of my previous eight victims were women. I don't hate women. I *love* women. Women are awesome. I dunno...maybe I was worried that a guy would kick my ass.

Anyway, after completing my seven-hour search for the perfect online phallus, it occurred to me that any healthy, straight woman with a working libido would want this dick. And my preference was to kill a filthy, disease-ridden whore. Really, I needed to send a picture of an unappealing dick—something tiny and weird-shaped and gross, so that any woman who wanted to meet up with me after seeing it would be deserving of her fate.

So I took a picture of my own dick.

Started sending it to various ladies in the area.

Most of them ignored me. It didn't hurt my feelings. I was used to being rejected, which is why I'd grown to hate women. No, I didn't mean that. Ignore that. That's not what I meant. I've already explained that women are great. They give birth!

I like to stab people. It's not my fault. God gave me a brain that wants to stab people, and are you going to tell Him that He messed up? Yes, the people I stab are women. Wouldn't it be more sexist to *not* stab women? Like, "Oh, no, I could never harm that helpless delicate flower!" No, I kill women because I believe that they should be able to take care of themselves!

I don't need to justify this to you. How do I know *you* don't stab women, huh? And when you're done stabbing them, you...I don't know, pee on them, or something.

I feel like I'm getting sidetracked. What I'm saying is that I sent dick pics to every wretched slut on the site. The ones who responded were generally unkind.

This plan wasn't going to work. I'd have to go back to my technique of killing extremely affordable prostitutes.

But then I got a reply.

You're fucking hot. Let's do this.

Millie

I sent the message, then leaned back against my chair still staring at the repulsive dick pic. I was mesmerized. How in the hell did such a small dick bend that way? And was that a...wart?

Jesus.

A guy sending images of that monstrosity out into the world deserved to die. I'd be doing the world a favor causing that—*thing*—to rot. Although I'm pretty sure it was already halfway there.

Was there a cock-rotting disease? I typed 'cock-rotting disease' into Google and found photos of infected dicks, the occasional pus-filled anus, and an oozing perineum or two. The series of symptoms was named after the French physician, Fournier, who'd first discovered them. Poor guy—his name forever associated with decaying taints.

But, no. That's not what my presumed future date—Mac—had. His was just small, discolored, deformed, and...oddly lumpy. If he thought I was touching that thing, except maybe to cut it off during his savage torture, he was sadly mistaken. And even then, I'd wear thick gloves.

Because *ew.*

I may be a ruthless serial killer, but I was still a girl. And I had fucking standards.

Unwilling to look at Mac's junk for even one more second, I closed the photo and noticed he'd replied back.

Hello, Millie!

You're also super attractive. Cool! Let's be intimate and stuff! Saturday at 8:00?

Lotsa love,

Mac

For fuck's sake, was he ten? Letting out a sigh and cursing the shit I had to do just to kill innocent people, I wrote back.

Send a pic of your face. I need to know who I'll be fuckin'.

I took my bulldog puppy, Manslaughter, out to pee. He snorted and sniffed and ran a few zoomies around the backyard before finally finding the perfect spot to do his business. When I came back inside, there was another message from Mac. The subject line simply read, "Me." I opened the attached photo and was pleasantly surprised. Yes, his male appendage clearly came from the deep bowels of hell, but he had a nice face. Kind eyes. A sweet smile.

Poor guy had no idea what he was in for. I couldn't wait to cut him.

I wrote back.

Saturday at 8:00 works. My place?

Assuming he'd agree, I sent him the address.

Now to prepare…

Mac

Heh heh. She was making it easy.

Almost *too* easy…

Nah. It wasn't a suspicious amount of easy. In today's slut-ridden society, women wanted penis so badly, they'd put their own personal safety at risk.

I'd assumed we'd have to meet in a public place first. I obviously couldn't stab her in the middle of a Cheddar's Scratch Kitchen, so it was always a pain when my victims wanted to meet somewhere with good lighting and other people around. Especially because they didn't always recognize my natural charm. The truth is, some women get a "skeevy" vibe from me. It pisses me off.

I bathe!

I groom!

What the hell is their problem? It makes me want to wrap my hands around their neck and squeeze until their eyeballs pop out.

43

Sorry about that. I promise I'm not an angry person. Also, no matter how hard you squeeze somebody's neck, their eyeballs don't pop out. I've tried.

Anyway, when she'd sent her address a few days ago, I'd looked it up and rejoiced. Not only was it a house and not an apartment, but she was in the middle of nowhere. No neighbors visible on Google Maps! Foolish girl! Didn't she realize how easy it would be to kill somebody in that environment? Poor, poor Millie. Tonight she would writhe in helpless torment as I stabbed her again and again and again and again, laughing at her inept attempts to escape.

Just to be clear, the fact that I would be treating Millie as an amalgam of all the women who'd rejected me does *not* mean I hate women. Some women are fine. Not my mom, but...waitresses, for example. I always tip them at least ten percent. I'd much rather have a woman be my server than a man, so let's keep the "Mac's a male chauvinist pig" talk to a minimum, okay?

On Saturday, I put on a clean T-shirt, combed my hair to hide the bald spot, washed my mustache, and put a switchblade knife in my pocket. Some killers, depraved freaks that they are, have a special weapon they use to claim their victims. Sometimes they even name it. Not me. I've got, like, nine or ten switchblades, and I didn't even think about which one I shoved into my pocket. My knife is not an extension of my penis.

I drove to her house. I had to go down a long, winding, dirt driveway to get there, which was completely surrounded by trees. Seriously, didn't she realize how much danger she was in? She could scream at the top of her lungs, and nobody would hear her. Hell, I could bury her corpse in these woods, and it would never be found. What a dumb bitch.

I parked, checked my mustache in the rearview mirror, then got out of the car. Stifling a giggle, I walked to her front door and knocked.

Millie

Smirking, I watched from my bedroom window as the balding fool walked toward my front door. He'd looked *way* better in his photo, which I'm guessing was at least a decade old. These days, Mac was sporting a crusty mustache, a dad bod, and a comb-over. Just...why? Didn't guys realize comb-overs were the leading cause of Sahara-like vaginas?

He was wearing a t-shirt with yellow stains near the armpits. He paired the classy shirt with some jeans and penny loafers.

Dear God...if ever a man needed to be put down, it was this one. Choking back laughter at how easy he'd made this for me, I checked my reflection in the floor-length mirror. Long red hair in a sleek ponytail. *Check.* Push-up bra in full effect. *Check.* Glossy lips. *Check.* I was dressed to kill.

And I planned to.

To him, I was just a girl looking to get laid. Innocent in my naivety for inviting him into my isolated home. Probably thinking he could fuck me six ways from Sunday because there were no neighbors around to hear me scream.

Heh.

As if I'd let his diseased organ anywhere near me.

As if he'd ever have the upper hand.

As if...as if...as if...

The doorbell rang. Spritzing a bit of perfume on my neck, I made my way downstairs. No weapons were concealed beneath my clothes. They were all in the bedside drawer. Most women kept vibrators, dildos, condoms, and lube there. I kept an ice pick, a butcher knife, a meat cleaver, the sharpest scissors I could find, a meat mallet, a Taser gun, and even some aerosol spray and a lighter.

I loved torture.

But not as much as the moment my victim's eyes went sightless in death.

It was better than sex.

Putting on my innocent game face, I pulled open the door. "Mac, hey! Nice to see you. Please come in."

He gave me a clownish smile and walked into my lair. Something green was stuck between his teeth. His eyes glimmered in the dim light of my home, one lonely lamp lighting the entirety of the downstairs. I could tell he liked what he saw. Why wouldn't he? I looked way fuckin' better than he did.

Smelled better too. Was that…refried beans? He leaned in for a hug, and I got the full-on Taco Bell experience. I wasn't convinced he'd recently eaten refried beans—it might very well have been his natural odor.

"Hi, Millie. Nice to meet you. If you don't mind me saying it, you sure are pretty."

I walked to the couch and spread out a blanket. I didn't want his aromatic ass anywhere near my velvet sofa. "Thanks. Please have a seat." I motioned to the newly-covered couch. "Would you like a drink? A scotch, maybe?"

"No alcohol, please. It makes me feel funny."

"How about a Shirley Temple?" If he said yes, I might not be able to withstand the urge to kill him right where he stood.

"A Shirley Temple would be grand!"

"A round of Shirley Temples coming right up!" I said, trying hard to control the urge to kick him in the balls, then laugh in his dimwitted face.

"Great. Thanks!" He looked relieved. "There's nothing wrong with a drink like that, right?"

"Nothing at all. Lots of grown men impress their dates by asking for a Shirley Temple."

Mac frowned. "Are you being sarcastic?"

"Not at all. That would be impolite." I walked into the kitchen before he could see my eyes tearing up with suppressed laughter. Mac sure as hell didn't have much going for him.

Carrying the drinks back into the living room, I handed him one and sat on the far end of the couch. The guacamole and sour cream stench rolling off him was getting to me.

Manslaughter, my bulldog, strutted into the room, muscular legs bowed, and panting heavily. He stood in front of Mac, sniffing him intently, probably enticed by my date's cologne—Mexican fiesta.

Mac's nervousness was apparent.

"Mac, meet my pooch." Manslaughter wrapped his paws around Mac's calves and began humping. The snorting intensified.

Mac, trying to gently shake the dog off his leg said, "Wow, your dog's a bit of a whore, isn't he?" He giggled timidly.

Appreciating his attempt at humor, I laughed. "Sorry about that. He's a pup and still a little rambunctious." I pulled Manslaughter off his leg, noticed the resulting white patch on his jeans, and lured the doggy into the guest bedroom with treats. After I got him settled in, I ventured back to the living room. Mac was sour-faced as he wiped at the wet spot on his jeans with a handkerchief. *He carried a handkerchief?* When he saw me, the pissy look was immediately replaced by and easy-going smile, but it was clear he wasn't as amused by Manslaughter's antics as he'd pretended to be.

Choosing to change the subject, I said, "So, Mac, what do you do for a living?"

"I'm a computer repairman."

Well, that tracked. I bet he liked D&D too. And had Bigfoot posters hanging on his wall.

"Nice. What do you do in your spare time?"

"Every Saturday night I play D&D with my friends. And I love horror movies and books."

"I love horror too. It's my favorite."

"Mine too."

"Favorite monster?" I asked.

"I love cryptids. Probably Mothman." *Close enough.*

47

He looked at me shyly and grinned, the green thing stuck between his teeth highlighted in the soft lamplight. "What about you? Do you have a favorite monster?"

I took a long drink from my Shirley Temple. I was fervently wishing I'd loaded it with alcohol. This was painful.

"I'm pretty partial to human monsters. They're the scariest of all."

His shy smile turned into a full-blown grin. "Damn right they are." He scooted closer to me on the couch.

I had him—hook, line, and sinker. And he *really* needed to die. I sat my drink down and asked, "Interested in joining me in my bedroom?"

Mac

See, this is why Millie needed to die. Her and her perverted dog.

What was wrong with a bit of courtship? Talking. Getting to know each other first. Making a personal connection before inviting me into the bedroom where dozens, if not hundreds, of other men had vigorously fornicated with her. I bet she even asked them for cunnilingus! Demanded it, more likely. Those poor men, choking back bile and holding their noses.

Would it have killed her to chat for fifteen or twenty minutes before we started removing clothing? No. What *would* kill her was her haste.

I mean, yes, I would have killed her even if she wanted to talk first, but my point is that women, in general, are vile, carnal creatures who deserve to be extinguished from existence.

"I am," I said. "I'm very interested. Your bedroom sounds like a happy place."

Millie smiled at me. For a split-second I wondered if her smile was sincere, but then I decided it totally was and followed her into her bedroom.

She'd chosen a strange décor—plastic wrap all over the walls and floor. Probably her idea of *feng shui* or whatever crap women thought about when they decorated. She had no idea she'd made my clean-up process easier.

I reached into my pocket, as though I were retrieving a condom. Most likely the diseased tramp would tell me no condom was necessary—she'd probably already acquired all the STDs she could get.

I pulled out the switchblade.

Millie's smile disappeared.

I pressed the button, and the blade snapped out.

"What the fuck?" she asked.

Oh, I'd show her what the fuck. I had, in the past, tried out various ways to inform my victims about why they were going to die, but, quite honestly, I wasn't good at remembering what I'd written out, and it was easier just to get right to the stabbing.

I thrust the knife at her, plunging it deep into the yielding flesh of her...no, wait. Shit, I'd missed! She grabbed a pillow off the bed and swung it at me. It was a firm pillow, and it was a surprisingly hefty swing from a helpless female. As it struck my hand, the knife went flying toward the wall.

I ran for my weapon.

Picking it up, I spun around and saw her opening a drawer. Ha! She probably thought she could subdue me by squirting lube into my eye.

She turned toward me brandishing a butcher knife.

I didn't even want to know what kind of kinky sex acts required her to keep a butcher knife in her bedside drawer. My God, was she depraved.

"If you put the knife down, I'll leave you unharmed," I said. (I was lying.)

Millie shook her head and gestured toward me. "Bring it."

Millie

What was this? The nerdy little twerp thought he could take *me* on? Was he completely braindead?

I sighed. This was not how I'd planned for the evening to go. I might have to work up a light sweat, which was bullshit. Dude was supposed to come to my house, be seduced by my many charms, allow himself to be tortured and mutilated, then go willingly to his basement death. Instead, he had this puny little switchblade, no doubt an extension of his penis, and I had to deal with his hyper-masculine bravado.

Ugh. Fuck my life!

I looked at him brandishing his dipshit knife and realized I'd chosen the wrong weapon. I wasn't gonna be like Mac, with his stainless-steel schlong. Once again, I strolled sedately to my nightstand and pulled open the drawer. Replacing the butcher knife in its case, I rifled through the rest of the contents until I wrapped my palm around the handle of the ice pick. It felt good. It felt... *right*. I straightened, intuitively knowing he didn't have the fortitude—or the balls—to attack a woman from behind. As I pricked the tip of my finger to check the razor blade sharpness of my chosen weapon, I let out a tinkling laugh and said softly, "You amuse me, little man."

"What's that supposed to mean? Little?" he huffed.

"I think you know." I turned, stared at his stupid face a little longer than intended (I'm pretty sure I lost a few IQ points during the brief interlude), jumped on the bed, and charged. As I leapt off the mattress, I plunged the ice pick into his flabby body. He managed to sidestep my attack, and the weapon harmlessly penetrated the fleshy part of his underarm. He let out a pained cry and whipped his knife across my abdomen, superficially cutting my skin.

Eh, whatever. Skin would heal. But the son-of-a-bitch *ruined* my black mini-dress. Pissed beyond belief that my brand new, very expensive dress was bound for the garbage pile, I let out a fierce roar.

He blinked with surprise, as if he'd never heard a woman roar before.

I charged at him. To give credit where it's due, he stood his ground. He dodged my ice pick attack and slashed the top of my arm, wrist to elbow.

"Fuck!" I shouted. It stung like hell, though I couldn't help but admire his skills. Any other guy would have had an ice pick protruding from his forehead following the sheer awesomeness of my athletic prowess.

Mac grinned, then punched me in the stomach.

I doubled over, stood back up, and punched him in the jaw as hard as I could.

He stumbled backward, collided with my bed, then stumbled forward—right into my swinging fist. His eyes crossed. Looking dizzy, he turned around and spat some blood onto my expensive velvet blanket.

Thoroughly pissed off, I stabbed my ice pick into his less-than-spectacular buttock. He groaned, gyrated, and performed a rather impressive, yet baffling, version of the moonwalk.

Then he ran into my bathroom, slammed the door, and flipped the lock.

I pounded on the heavy wood. "Open up, you chickenshit!"

No response.

"Mac, goddammit, I have a key. Try to keep some of your dignity, and open the fucking door!"

I heard cabinet doors opening and closing. Then, "Uh, Millie? Do you have hydrogen peroxide and bandages? I don't want these puncture wounds to get infected."

I stood there, open-mouthed. He'd stopped trying to kill me so he could disinfect his wounds?

"What the fuck?" I whispered.

Deciding to play it cool, I said, "Yeah, in the cabinet above the toilet."

"Cool, thanks."

"Mac, uh, why did you dance after I stabbed you?"

"To distract you so I could get away."

I nodded. "That's fair. Good job."

"I've been doing this for a long time."

"Really?" He'd once again shocked me into silence. "You're a…killer?"

"Yeah. Are you? Most ladies I know don't have ice picks in their night table. Or their entire boudoir covered in plastic sheeting."

"Why don't you open the door, and we'll discuss this like the psychotic adults we are."

I heard him hiss in pain and assumed he was using the peroxide.

"Okay. Just give me a minute." More hissing and a whispered, "Ow! Ow! Ow!" came from behind the door.

I walked to the bed and sat down.

Several minutes later, Mac poked his head out. He looked at me. I looked at him. Yeah, he was a total buffoon, but…

"Maybe we should work together," I heard myself say.

Mac

"Is that a joke?" I asked.

"No," Millie said.

"Is it a trap?"

"No."

I opened the door all the way. Millie stood there, letting the blood run down her arm. It was surprisingly sexy.

"Then what exactly do you mean?"

She shrugged. It was a surprisingly sexy shrug. Maybe I just found her sexy overall. I mean, she definitely looked less like an oozing, scab-covered whore than I anticipated.

"You have a desire to kill," said Millie. "I have a desire to kill. I think it would be nice to team up and commit murder with somebody who understands. I don't know about you, but since I'm trying not to get caught, I can't really chat with anyone about it afterward."

I thought about her words. It *would* be nice to have a friend who could relate to the darkness in my heart. We could slaughter a victim, then spoon in bed while we reminisced.

"We couldn't fuck on top of the corpse afterward," I said.

"I would never ask you to do that."

"I'm serious. It's a deal-breaker."

"I completely get it."

"And, uh, the victim has to be female."

"Why? You hate women?"

"Yes. I mean, no. Women are awesome. They make the world go round. It's just my *modus operandi*, and what kind of a serial killer would I be if I veered from my *modus operandi*? I'm not an incel or anything like that. I just don't want to kill a dude."

"That's fine," said Millie. "I'll kill anything. I'm basically pansexual with murder. Also, I'm pansexual."

"That's good to know," I lied.

"Did you have a backup victim for tonight?"

"No," I admitted. "I sent my dick pic all over the place, but you were the only one who was interested. Only, now I know you weren't *really* interested."

"Well, Mac, I'm going to deliver a harsh truth. You do not have a good penis."

"I know."

"I have plenty of options. Mostly guys, but some women, too. I could set up a booty call in five minutes. Do you want to tag along?"

"I do," I said. "I really do."

She was right. It literally took five minutes for her to set up a date with a woman who was interested in unnaturally wicked carnality. "She'll be here in twenty minutes," Millie told me.

"Wow. You're efficient."

"I'm a hot woman. This was not a big challenge."

"How are we going to do this?"

"When she gets here, I'm going to loosen her up with a couple of drinks. You're going to hide in the closet. I'll bring her into the bedroom, and you can whack off, or whatever you want to do, while you watch us through the gap. After I knock her out, come out and help me carry her into the basement. But you're helping me get rid of the body afterward—you don't get to enjoy the fun and then skip out on the cleanup."

"I love this idea," I said.

About half an hour later, Millie came into the bedroom with a heavily tattooed girl whose hair was long and purple. They kissed. My stomach churned at the sight. Disfiguring your skin with ink was vile. Spitting in the face of God by changing the color He'd chosen for your hair was vile. And *two* women expressing their sexuality went beyond vile! It was absolutely disgusting.

"Disgusting" was worse than "vile," right? I suppose it didn't matter.

They lay on the bed, kissing and groping for way too long. When was Millie going to get to the bloodshed?

The girl looked over at the closet. "Is somebody in there?"

Millie slammed her hand over the girl's mouth.

Millie

I glared at the girl, Taylor, whose green eyes stared back at me in confusion and fear. My pussy was wet and achy—I wanted her badly—and it kind of excited me that Mac was watching. I'd never had sex, or taken a human life, with somebody watching.

54

"You bite my hand, it will be the last thing you ever do," I whispered forcefully into her ear. I couldn't stop myself from rubbing against her leg. God, I was turned on.

Too turned on. I wasn't sure I could keep myself from hurting her, and I didn't want to make a mess on my bed…at least, not that kind of mess. I needed to skip the sex and move to the torture.

I punched Taylor in the face, knocking her out. Usually this took a few punches, or some Chloroform, so I was pleased with myself.

Mac emerged from the closet. He didn't seem to be hard, but maybe his nasty little dick simply didn't put a noticeable bulge in his pants.

"Carry her downstairs to the basement workroom," I said. "Use the handcuffs on the workbench to restrain her wrists and ankles. I'll be down in a few minutes."

"What are you going to do in the meantime?"

"What do you *think* I'm going to do?"

"I have no idea."

"Use your imagination. Hurry before she wakes up."

"Fine." Mac picked up my almost-lover and carried her out of the room. I stared at the departing figures and wondered if I'd lost my damn mind, doing this with a partner. Could I trust him?

Pushing the thought aside, I grabbed my vibrator from the *other* bedside drawer and went into the bathroom. Seconds later, there was screaming…but not the painful kind.

I walked down the stairs. Taylor was bound on the floor, still unconscious, and Mac was anxiously pacing. I was glad that he'd waited for me—I'd half-expected to enter my workroom and find Taylor's headless corpse, which *really* would've pissed me off.

With Mac's help, I removed her dress and panties, and then we hauled the limp body toward the throne.

Oh, yeah, I've got a throne in my basement. It's wonderful.

"When we sit her on this, she's going to wake up screaming bloody murder and trying to get away," I explained. "I need you to restrain her while I get her locked in."

Mac nodded.

We lifted our poor victim into a standing position, then I cheerfully shoved Taylor's body onto the throne. As she landed on the spiked seat—did I mention it had a spiked seat? —her eyes opened and anguished screams tore from her throat. "Grab her shoulders," I demanded. "Don't let her get up!"

Mac did as he was told while I fastened iron clamps around Taylor's neck, chest, and shins. As her weight settled evenly onto the half-inch spikes, the sharp metal ground into her tender flesh, and cherry red drops of blood dripped onto the cement...and the wood piled beneath the iron chair.

Flipping a switch, the industrial vent above the chair turned on. I doused the wood in lighter fluid and tossed on a lit match. The logs immediately caught fire. I slapped a piece of duct tape over her mouth.

"What is all this?" Mac asked. "I thought we were going to kill her."

"Oh, we are. But we have to get all the fun and excitement out of it we can, Mac!" Taylor was squirming uncomfortably. "It's all about the torture." My fingers found their way between my legs, and I came within seconds. I wondered if Mac had ever even seen a woman orgasm in real life. He struck me as more of a—love 'em and leave 'em frustrated and unsatisfied, while they secretly wished for him to go far away so they could use their vibrator in peace—kind of guy.

I pointed to the seat of the iron chair, which now had a decidedly orange hue from the heat. "Pretty cool, huh?"

Mac shrugged.

A couple of minutes later, I sniffed the air which was redolent with the aroma of freshly grilled human skin. Ahhhh. Better than the finest perfume.

As Taylor burned, I began roughly yanking out clumps of her chestnut-colored hair and throwing them onto the fire. When I got tired of that, I unclamped the restraints and lifted her from the chair. The ripping sound her skin made as I pulled her into a standing position was grotesque, as were the layers of skin still cooking on the spiked seat. The backs of her legs and buttocks were a reddened, slimy, blistered, leaking mess.

I tossed her onto the pad I'd placed on the floor, stained with the blood of dozens of victims. She landed with a loud thud, followed by an agonized groan. I studied her. Despite the missing layers of skin, her ass was still lush as fuck. I shed my slashed and bloodied dress as I made my way to the supply cabinet, then slid the strap-on dildo over my pelvis. It grazed gently against my swollen clit. Without giving Mac a second thought, I rolled Taylor onto her stomach and fucked her mangled ass, my pent-up desires causing my aggressions to take hold.

God, she felt good. As I thrust into her, I felt something igniting inside me. It built and built until the ultimate explosion sent stars careening across my vision. Pulling out, I flopped beside her on the mat, struggling to catch my breath.

Feeling energized, I sat Taylor up and leaned her against the wall. She moaned as her nearly skinless bottom was dragged across the mat. I put the strap-on back in the cabinet and pulled out a contraption I'd just purchased. I couldn't wait to try it!

It was basically a large, centrally located golden hoop attached to four equally spaced nylon cords. At the end of each cord were softball sized golden hoops. Those four hoops were made like septum piercing rings. You opened them up, pushed them through the skin, then clasped them shut again.

That's exactly what I did.

I pushed a hoop through one side of Taylor's breast and out the other side, locked it, and repeated the steps on her other breast. Removing the ankle cuffs, I put the soles of her feet flat on the floor, and pushed her knees toward her chest. Then I did the same thing to her ankles. A hoop stabbed just above the ankle bone came out the other side, and the lock popped into place at the back of her leg, a process I repeated on the opposite ankle. It was fun! She looked so beautiful sitting there huddled on the floor, blood running in heavy rivulets from the flesh piercings, and completely unable to straighten her legs. If she did, she'd pull those pretty golden hoops right through the front of her breasts, tearing through her nipples and leaving gaping, bloody slit-wounds in both tits.

Realizing her predicament, large tears ran down her cheeks, and her breaths came in ragged gasps. That shit had zero effect on me. Taylor was nothing more than a piece of meat.

I turned on some catchy music, "Johnny B. Goode" by Chuck Berry, and went to work with one of my favorite devices…the "Pear of Anguish." In its base position, its shape resembled a pear—a wide bottom that gradually narrowed. The metal at the top was divided into four petal-shaped segments that opened when the lever at the opposite end was turned. I inserted the closed petals into her pussy and began cranking the lever, my excitement overtaking everything. I cranked harder and faster.

At first, Taylor seemed ambivalent. But as the metal petals began expanding—tearing through her vaginal walls and cervix, destroying her fallopian tubes and ovaries, annihilating her uterus—she passed out from the pain. I pulled the instrument out without deflating it first. Chunks of bloody, pink flesh clung to the petals.

Figuring she'd want a cigarette after such a satisfying experience—I sure as hell did—I grabbed my scalpel and made a deep incision over her jaw, exposing the molars at the back of her mouth. Tucking a lit Marlboro between them, I also lit one for myself. We smoked them together, as ashes fell upon her pale, waxy skin.

I checked her pulse. It was thready and weak but still there. She was alive, and I knew exactly what I wanted to do for the big finish. Dragging her tiny frame out of my basement and into a clearing behind my house, which caused the golden hoops to rip out the Achilles tendons in both her legs, I tied her to a stake surrounded by wood. Once I had the fire burning brightly, I relaxed in the hammock I'd placed there strictly for bodies-burning-alive viewing purposes.

Most likely, Taylor would die from smoke inhalation before she'd feel the fire licking against her skin, which was a real shame. Burning was an utterly agonizing death, and one I enjoyed watching.

I got lucky.

Taylor was conscious throughout the entire process. Even when her skin's dermis cracked open and melted fat poured from the crevices. Even when her eyeballs exploded within their sockets from the heat. Even as the heat scorched her lungs and made breathing painful and impossible. She remained conscious until the shrinkage of the skin around her neck became severe enough to strangle her to death.

It was beautiful.

I lounged in my hammock long after she'd died, watching chunks of her skin fall into the flames. When the fire was nothing more than coals, I went back inside the house, satisfied by a job well done.

Mac was standing there, his face pale, his mouth agape.

"Uhhhhhh…" he said.

Mac

What the fuck?

Seriously, what the fuck?

What? The? Fuck?

Killing filthy whores was a satisfying experience. Slash their throat, watch the lifeforce drain from their body, and move on. What Millie had done was…it was…it was *messed up!* It was depraved! The woman was batshit crazy!

"What's wrong?" Millie asked. "Are you upset that I finished the job without you? Nobody told you to stay in the house."

"You…you…you…uhhh…you…"

"Yes, Mac? Use your words."

"That was…that was *not* the behavior of a mentally healthy person."

"What exactly did you think I was going to do?"

"Kill her! Stab, stab, stab!" He mimed this action. "I didn't know that you'd, like, burn up her ass, or, like, use that hoop thing! You played with yourself! Right there in front of me *and* her!"

"You don't get sexual satisfaction from this sort of thing?"

"Of course not! That's deviant! You're a deviant! You're the biggest deviant I've ever met! My God! How do you sleep at night? How do you look in the mirror and not smash it with your fist because the sight of yourself fills you with a deep and intense self-loathing? You're a sick woman, Millie! You need help!"

"The message I'm getting is that our collaboration didn't work out for you."

"There was no collaboration! That was all you! I don't think you even realized I was there most of the time!"

"Okay, that's true," Millie admitted. "I got caught up in the experience. But you could've helped. You could have fingered her while she was burning."

"That's disgusting! This is why I hate women! This, right here, is exactly why I think all women should die."

"You still have to help me clean up."

"I'm not cleaning up a goddamn thing, you perverted, foul, wretched—"

Millie took a step toward me. "Are we going to have to fight this out?"

"Maybe we are," I said. "Do you really think you can beat me?"

As it turned out, she could.

To be fair, after she kicked me in the balls, I didn't really stand a chance. I've been kicked in the balls before, but never so hard that one of them popped. From that point forward, I wasn't able to put up much of a fight.

The throne was every bit as unpleasant as it looked when the purple-haired girl was on it. But not as unpleasant as the flaying that followed.

And when she got started on the serious genital mutilation, wearing thick gloves, I longed for the time when a popped testicle was the worst of my problems.

I begged her to kill me. She promised she would, but only after we wrote our story, as a souvenir of the evening we spent together. She wanted the honest, uncensored truth, so that maybe she could fulfill her dream of being a published author.

"Make it entertaining as fuck," she warned me, "or I'll put very sharp, spiky things up your blistered ass."

I've done my best. It's taken a while, because I only have one finger left to type with, but I think we've reached the end of this saga. I'm hoping she'll finally put me out of my misery. Goodnight, whoever is reading this, and thank you for your attention.

Millie

Good job, Mac.
    But I'm still putting sharp and spiky things up your ass.

GPS
Glenn Rolfe

"You don't know whether you're capable of murder until it's a matter of life or death."

This was the bullshit emanating from the backseat of Maggie's RAV 4 as they made their way up I-84.

Blake shut up about murder long enough to poke his head between the front seats. "Why are we getting off already?"

Jackson held up a hand, his sudden irritation with his best friend finding its way out. "The GPS said Exit 16."

"No way, bro. She's busted. It's too soon. You don't get off 84 until Hartford, or right after."

"The GPS says 16, we're taking 16. Now, can you shut the fuck up for a minute?"

Blake flopped back and let out a *pfft* sound.

Merge onto 188 South.

"Did you hear that, Blake? She says to merge on to 188. Does that work? Is that all right with you?"

"Whatever. That dumb bitch is taking us off course."

Maggie sipped from her water bottle before setting the travel mug between her legs and leaning her head against the passenger window. "I have a headache," she said. "Can you guys give it a rest?"

Jackson reached over and placed a hand on her thigh. Her hand enfolded his as she closed her eyes.

Jackson was grateful for the moment of silence. Blake almost never shut up which is why he made a good companion on road trips. He always had something to say, the conversations helped to keep you awake on long stretches of highway, especially at night. But right now, Jackson, and Maggie apparently, wanted some good old-fashion quiet.

He recalled something called the Quiet Game that his aunt Janet and Uncle Pete used to make him, and his cousins play on their summer trips to Old Orchard Beach, Maine. The game had something to do with pilgrims and seeing how long you could go without speaking. If you talked, you had to pay a forfeit. The thought of pilgrims brought frightening images to Jackson's mind. He never liked their black and white attire. Maybe it was all the Salem witch stuff or the senseless killings of American Natives. Whatever the case, he never trusted them and even as a kid on those long summer beach drives, he was certain the forfeit would be the lobbing off one body part or another, be it the tongue or a hand. It would certainly be more than a slap on the wrist.

188 South led to Munn Road before the GPS directed him to take Jeremy Swamp Road.

Jackson's companions had fallen asleep. He heard Maggie's soft, slow breathing, beside him, and Blake's strange wheezy snore coming from behind him. As much as he liked some quiet night driving, the tongue stealing pilgrims were stalking the front of his mind.

Taking you off course...

Blake's insistence that the GPS was going off the rails echoed as Jackson guided the RAV 4 down the dark stretch of road with the odd name.

Jeremy Swamp Road.

The trees encroaching the slim backroad were thick. The pitch-black pavement appeared to narrow even further as he rubbed his eyes, certainly his sudden freaked out state of mind was playing tricks on him. This moment was like some warped reality, a *Twilight Zone* entry. Jackson wished he'd listened to Blake about staying on 84 longer, even if he was wrong. Before he could turn the car around and head back toward the highway, the dashboard lights flickered.

The acceleration weakened as if the car were out of gas—impossible since thy just filled up at the last service plaza—or like the time the fuel pump went in his friend Paul's hundred-dollar Chrysler, dubbed "The Falcon". He and Paul had been stranded out near Owens Lake. The area had supposedly been haunted by a lake monster. Paul's dad warned them against driving the piece of shit car anywhere, but they roared out into the great unknown screaming "freedom" at the tops of their lungs like Mad Max in that Braveheart movie. They were never eaten by a creature from the lake, just sidelined by the bad fuel pump, and ended up being rescued by Paul's dad after calling him from a payphone outside a place called the Village Inn. The Falcon never made it home again, returning Jackson and Paul to foot soldiers dependent upon their parents as escorts.

The dash lights of the RAV4 flickered into a steady strobe-light rhythm. In the headlights, something darted across the road. Something that looked more like a someone, someone short with a funny shaped head.

Now, you're really losing it.

The headlamps flickered and went out completely, along with the interior lights. The RAV4 died. The power steering was gone, so Jackson did his best to crank the wheel and guide the vehicle to the shoulder of the road. The RAV4 rolled to a stop with only the front wheels off the blacktop.

Jackson did his best to keep from freaking out as he tried to look out the windows to see what had crossed the road.

It was a deer.

Only that wasn't even close to the truth. Deer don't have arms and legs. They don't have giant round heads, either.

Maggie raised her head, a hand to her neck. "What's going on?" she said.

"I'm not sure. The car just...died."

"What? Where are we?" she added.

"That goddam Global Positioning Succubus," Blake said from the shadow behind them.

Jackson gnashed his teeth, resisting the very strong urge to tell Blake to shut up.

"Yeah, I don't know. We're on a back road." Jackson didn't mention seeing whatever the hell it was he saw crossing the street.

A deer.

"No shit," Blake muttered.

Maggie turned to face the back seat. "Blake, stop." She reached into the center console and grabbed her cellphone. "I have AAA. We'll at least get to the nearest motel."

A loud thwack against the back of the car startled them.

"What the fuck was that?" Blake yelped, sticking his head between the front seats. Jackson couldn't make out his friend's face in the darkness, but there was a quiver in Blake's voice that unnerved him.

"Something just hit the back of the car," Maggie said, her phone forgotten in her hand.

"You better have some fucking weapons in here," Blake said.

Just a deer.

Deer don't hit your car after you stop.

66

Beyond the windows, the entire night was like a black hole—vacant, eternal nothingness. Even the light from the moon was blocked out. Jackson tried to start the car. The keys turned in the ignition, but the vehicle gave zero response.

"Jesus!" Maggie cried and flung herself back against Jackson.

"What? What the fuck is it?" Jackson said.

"Someone was just right there with its face to my window."

"Fuck!" Blake kicked at his window.

The back door opened. Blake screamed as he tried to climb closer to Jackson and Maggie in the front.

"Shit," Blake screamed. "Fucking shit, it's got my leg!"

"What? What does?" Jackson said.

Blake was jerked violently out of the car.

"Jackson!" he screamed on his way out into the night.

Jackson pushed his own door open and grabbed Maggie's wrist, pulling her after him. "Come on, come on!" he said.

Maggie gasped.

Jackson spilled onto the pavement. He pulled at Maggie's arm, but she was stuck.

"Get off me!" she said.

Jackson scrambled to his feet and saw one of the small shapes taking Maggie's heel in the face. He grabbed both of her hands and pulled her out next to him.

They got to their feet and ran, booking it down Jeremy Swamp Road, racing back the way they came.

Jackson heard footfalls in pursuit. He didn't dare to look back. He didn't want to see one of those things. He thought of his best friend. Obnoxious or not, he'd known Blake since they were eight years old. His legs slowed.

"What are you doing?" Maggie said.

"Blake."

"No, no, no, honey, he's dead. We're next if we stop."

"You go, run, don't look back."

"What? No way. No fucking way Jackson. I'm not leaving without you."

"Then you know I can't just leave Blake here with… them."

He stopped.

Maggie ran five more steps before she did the same. "Goddamn it, Jackson."

Jackson turned, feet spread, fists up. He didn't know who or what was coming, but he wasn't leaving his friend out here without a fight.

The night was cooler but not cold. Summer was in retreat but even with the first fallen leaf being a couple weeks away, the warmth was clinging on for dear life.

Jackson wished the clouds would break, even long enough for them to see their attackers positions.

"Get behind me," he said.

He felt Maggie's hand on his shoulder.

"Where are they?" she whispered.

He'd heard them, multiple feet scurrying in pursuit. Now, the night was deathly quiet. Jackson stepped forward; Maggie kept a hand on his back.

"Blake," he called.

"What are you doing?" Maggie said.

"We have to know if he's all right. We're not hiding. They know where we are."

"Blake," Jackson said again. "If you're ok, say something."

Feet skittered across the blacktop behind them.

"Shit," Maggie said. "They're all around us."

"Motherfuckers," he muttered. "Blake!"

Hight-pitched laughter, like metal tines scraping porcelain plates, split the night.

He's dead.

"Okay, shit, yeah, we need to get the hell out of here," Jackson whispered.

Maggie clutched his shoulders as the small figures in the darkness closed in, closer and closer. "I told you we should have run. Now, we're fucked."

"Fuck that," Jackson said. "Don't talk like that. We're not dying here. Not tonight."

Maggie's scream in Jackson's ear dropped his stomach to his ankles. Jackson's knees buckled as she stumbled over him, her shrieks coming in full-blown ear-piercing wails.

The things closed in upon them. Jackson lie on the pavement. He could see tufts of wild hair sprouting from the tops and sides of their bulbous heads, heads too large to be human set upon child-like bodies.

Maggie was yanked away and dragged from the road before he could find out whether she was hurt.

Jackson tried to rise, but claws slashed his cheek, the side of his neck. He rolled over, face down in the road and covered his head with his arms, protecting his face and neck. Headlights in the distance blossomed to life. He could feel the warmth of his blood gushing from where his attackers cut him. Two strong hands clutched his ankles.

"No, please, no!"

The approaching vehicle's lights grew. Jackson could hear its engine.

"Jackson!"

"Maggie!" he cried in response as he the tar beneath his face scraped his already rend flesh.

The gathering creatures snickered like a pack of hyenas unafraid of him or the approaching vehicle. Two more grabbed his wrists as he was lifted from the ground, a small grace as he was hauled from the back street and carried away.

"Maggie!" he screamed.

A claw dug into his scalp as one of them clutched him by the hair causing Jackson to groan.

The car slowed as it passed them. Brake lights like a red room special came to life on the road above them.

"Help!" Jackson said.

He was violently thrown to the ground, his collarbone slamming against a rock jutting up from the grass. Heat flooded the area between his shoulder and neck. His skin went clammy as his stomach curdled.

"Hey, is somebody out there?"

A man's voice from the road.

Filthy little sausage-like fingers slipped past his lips and down his throat. The taste of mud and rotten vegetation filled his mouth as he gagged against the intrusive digits.

Jackson was lifted into the air and driven down hard, his head slamming into the ground. The night went sideways. A ringing in his ears drowned out any sounds around him. Jackson's vision doubled, his eyes floating in their sockets.

He was carried deeper into the woods, the dark world around him a tunnel of shapes and shadows. The bizarre creatures' clawed hands continued to grip and regrip his appendages as he was taken further from civilization and the road with the stupid name.

He had no idea if Maggie or Blake were with him, or whether either of them were still alive. The muffled sounds came clear as the grunts and snorts of his captors grew louder.

Could these things talk? Would they punish him for trying to communicate?

The hands released him into the air. Jackson fell, his hands reaching out at nothing for a number of seconds until his shoulder and hip came down hard. He tumbled downhill, one ankle snapping, his skin broken, the busted bone in his lower leg exposed after striking a tree, his face rolled over thorns until his body came to a stop before a campfire.

Jackson struggled to raise his swimming head to take in his surroundings. He instantly regretted surviving the fall.

There were hundreds of small-bodied, big-headed things lining the mouth of a cave less than fifty yards away. Several of them were dragging two more bodies—Maggie and Blake—toward the fire.

He tried to speak up, but barely managed an audible groan.

With one shaky palm, Jackson pressed against the ground, but pain exploded from numerous spots on his broken body. He collapsed back to the ground. His ankle and collarbone were fucked.

"Puh-puh-please…" Maggie said.

One of his eyes was swollen shut as he watched four of the big-headed creatures grab her by each appendage. His mind comprehended what was about to happen before the rest of him was ready to accept it. The four creatures were tiny in stature but far from meek. Their corded muscles flexed and bulged in the firelight as they pulled.

Maggie's screech into the night pierced his heart and sent an engorged fear through his body. His ass puckered and for the briefest of infinitesimal seconds Jackson was certain he would shit himself. The two creatures tugging on Maggie's arms fell to their rumps as they tore the appendages from her body. Maggie fell silent as the back of her head hit the ground.

Jackson prayed she was dead, but more than that he begged whatever God or gods ruled this world that he might be spared of any kind of gruesome ending. It felt shameful and selfish but to hell with it. The feeling swallowing him was so fucking far beyond any kind of fear he'd ever known.

Beyond Maggie's dismembered body, he saw Blake being raised, a spear through his body, the tip protruding from his mouth. Jackson didn't have to see the entry point to know his plea for mercy from these horrible beings was not going to be granted.

What were they? How long have they been here, doing this, killing and mutilating people? How had they gotten away with it?

He saw the meat hook coming straight at him before it smashed his two front teeth, and punctured the roof of his mouth.

Brief synoptic flashes of Maggie's face, her smile, her blue eyes, her hips. The road he grew up on. His dad. His mom. His black boots.

Maggie awoke. Despite being able to feel them, her arms were gone. She sat naked. Her right leg was gone from the knee down. She tried to scream but her lips were sutured shut.

Across from her three melon-headed young creatures fondled each other as they gazed upon her deformed body. Lust and hunger in their crooked eyes.

I don't want this.
I don't want this.
Please, kill me.
Kill me.

The perverted younglings giggled as they edged closer and closer.

Maggie's screams filled the cave. Somewhere back on Jeremy Swamp Road, the creatures waited for their next victim.

Blue-Plate Special
Wile E. Young

"Ordering! I need four blowout patches, two dots and a dash, and a hot blonde in the sand!" I shouted through the long bar window where I could see Bobby slaving away at the skillet.

He twirled his spatula in a salute that he'd heard me before starting on the batter for the pancakes. The hours between 2:00 and 3:00 A.M. were the drag along times, you could only drink so much coffee.

The old Bannon coffee maker bubbled; I kept the hot plate going throughout my shift, even if we only saw a dozen people at most overnight. I poured the liquid into a white mug and hefted the pot, relishing the smell and reminding myself to pour a cup when I returned. The jukebox-sized radio was playing Jimi Hendrix's "All Along the Watchtower". There weren't many stations to pick up out here in the neon oasis we had created.

The barren stretches around the Salton were devoid of pretty much anything, so in the evening and night, you could pick out the JUNIPER FLAVOR DINER easily.

Besides headlights and the stars, it was the only beacon of light in the expanse.

Harvey Doyle grabbed at the mug after I finished pouring. "Thank you, Ms. Leah."

I smiled. "Anytime, Harvey. Good day?"

He waved his hands, fingerless gloves stained with paint from whatever project he was working on. "Found another wreck out on the north shore, plenty of scrap to work with."

The Salton Sea was a hop and a skip to the south of us, and every weekend Harvey spent his time combing the shore for the remnants of the glorious 60's left to bleach in the poisonous mud.

"It's a new piece, they drove all the way down from Portland for it," he said proudly, producing three polaroids from inside his coat. The pictures revealed some kind of twisting thing of metal, surrealist art that I couldn't understand, but that Harvey made his living on.

The OPEN sign on the other side of the window bathed its neon touch on the photos that made me think it was some alien monument on some distant planet. Harvey was waiting for my reaction, eager eyes searching for my approval.

I smiled and patted the old hippie on the shoulder. "Looks great and hopefully gets me bigger tips when you come through."

We both shared a laugh and I left him to his celebratory coffee. This was the upswing for Harvey; when he was sculpting, he could be a mean drunk. He didn't have a car, didn't believe in polluting the environment after his childhood on the Salton Sea, so the diner was a checkpoint on his excursions.

Picking up the half empty pot, I headed to the other end of the Juniper, where a woman in a flannel jacket was busy finishing off the last of the two omelets and hashbrowns she'd ordered.

"Can I get you anything else, Cathy?" I asked.

The trucker leaned back in her seat, flapping her cap to get some air. "Just some coffee. These hauls are getting to me."

I poured her a cup, wondering if she was coming from Phoenix or back from L.A.. Her rig sat out in the parking lot at the edge of the light, trailer attached. She'd been a regular on the night shifts for as long as I'd been working, always ordering the same thing when she passed through, and always complaining about the ancient air conditioning that barely dispelled the heat.

"How long have I been seeing you here, Leah? Eight years? Or is it Ten?" she asked, wiping a hand across her brow and sending fresh sweat droplets flying.

I poured the last of the pot and she drained the black java without care. "Close, Cath. Nine years this August."

The woman sighed, taking another long gulp. I wondered if her raspy voice was due to a smoking habit or scarring from the scalding coffee she seemed to gulp down.

"Never thought I'd be at this for thirty years." she said, replacing the cap and covering her gray hair, staring at the flatscreen Benny had installed a few years back. I didn't understand why he had gone out of the way to get a good model; there wasn't much to pick up out here except news affiliates and the occasional 80's movie rerun.

I left Cathy to her coffee, sliding the ticket onto the table as subtly as I could. She had a way of ruminating over her drink before she headed out onto her route and didn't like to be interrupted in it. A roughly drunkard-sized hole through the glass window was a testament to that.

We'd put plywood up over the section until we could get a new window. Cathy had offered to pay for the damages, but Benny had stood firm that we could wring Mr. Inebriation for all that he was worth.

Looking out of the diner windows was like looking at the ocean at night, beyond the ring of light there was nothing but darkness that ended in mountains and the faint stars where the sky met the horizon.

I saw a pair of yellow headlights in the distance. They came up fast and passed the diner just as quick, rocketing down Highway 111, probably heading into the San Bernardino valley.

Once upon a time, I'd been a girl with dreams who'd come out here for college and taken a job at a shitty diner an hour away from her apartment. It was just a temporary thing I had told myself, still did really, despite the lack of success. A few commercials, a few minor roles, but the reflection in the window had more grey hair than it did yesterday.

Never thought I would be doing this for thirty years…

Another twenty years and I could say the same.

"Hey! Waitress! Can we get some more coffee?" The kid called.

I stiffened, the flare of anger burning bright in my chest. I just wanted to walk over and slap the teenage bastard. There were four of them crammed into the booth at the back corner under the tv, my juniors by a decade or more, and unaware of the brick wall of life that was coming. I plastered on my best smile, holding up the empty coffee pot. "Just a minute."

They weren't even paying attention anymore, continuing whatever talk was considered good conversation at two in the morning. I tried to take pity. It hadn't been that long ago my girlfriends and I had been driving around in the middle of the night feeling infinite.

I placed the pot back on the warming plate, and pushed my way back through the double doors and immediately felt the swelter from the deep fryers. A new AC unit for the kitchen was always top of the list for Benny before something else broke and the fan fund became the "keep us afloat" cash.

Benny barely glanced over at me as I sunk into the small office chair behind the haggard IBM that functioned as our office. I'd set up a fan that blew a small stream of air that was only cold because of the bag of ice I'd put in front of it.

Benny flipped a pancake. "Food's almost ready and I don't want the coffee to burn." It wasn't said unkindly. He knew that if I sat down long enough in this chair, that I would slip off into a nice nap resting against my palm.

"I'll get it in a minute… Can I ask you a question?"

I saw him frown. Our relationship wasn't really based on asking questions; after nine years we kind of just accepted things as they were.

"Sure," he replied, shoveling the pancakes off onto a waiting plate before cracking two eggs and running the yolk across the griddle.

"Did I miss my shot? Is this it?"

He pursed his lips together, swirling the eggs in a scramble. "Do you think I missed my shot? That I'm not happy with my life?"

I gave him a small bemused smile. "I don't know, are you?"

He chuckled, a deep and happy sound. He gestured around the interior of the kitchen with his spatula. "Honestly, this is all I ever wanted. There's a simplicity in it, no complications. I meet good people, serve better food, and the world keeps turning."

The eggs came off the griddle and onto the plate. He wiped a bead of sweat from his hairy arm and looked at me fully. "There's not an easy answer, Leah. Other than go find the simplicity for yourself. You're not like me, comfort isn't in your bones, but throwing caution and chasing the sun is."

He went back to his own work, but he kept an eye on me.

I'm not sure what I would have told him, if I would have hung up my apron, told him goodbye and left the oasis of light behind. I like to think that I would have.

Instead, the back door banged open, bringing a blast of sweltering desert air, and the night shift busboy, Evan, came in swigging a bottle of water as he shut the door behind him.

Benny eyed the busboy, rolling his head towards the dining room. "I think Cathy is about to leave. You can start on her table as soon as she's finished."

Evan replaced his hat over his thick mane of brown hair and hoisted the portable radio he carried around while he worked. "Right, on it, but listen to this."

He unplugged the pair of headphones and turned the dial on the volume. For a second there was nothing but the static of empty air waves as the receiving set searched, then it whined and caught a new sound.

There were thumps, rhythmic and repeating every half-second, squeals that varied in tone and intensity. It hurt my ears to listen to and I saw Benny wave a hand. "Turn it off."

Evan reluctantly complied and the noise vanished back into the ether. Benny looked between the two of us as Evan joined me, leaning against the counter. "Sounds like an old numbers station. Used to listen to them when I was kid. Russian transmissions they sent to their people spying on us. There's still a few transmitting, I think."

Evan laughed. "Maybe it's just me, boss, but don't numbers stations usually send out numbers?"

Benny gestured with his spatula to the door. "It's just you, now go bus some tables."

Evan gave a halfhearted salute and pushed through the door. I followed him, thinking about Benny's advice.

"Order up!" Benny shouted, breaking me out of my meditation. I grabbed the coffee pot as I passed, feeling the heat even through the handle.

"Here you go, Harvey," I said, filling his already-empty mug up, but he didn't respond to me. He was looking at the radio at the other end of the room, the one that was supposed to be playing KBKI's finest 80's classics. But Aerosmith had disappeared, replaced with what sounded like high-pitched beeping coming in alternating tones and pitches. How long had this been playing? It couldn't have been that long; my sojourn in the back had barely taken five minutes.

The sounds were… calming… in a way. It was lucky that I had gotten Harvey's food on the table before I'd noticed. My arms relaxed, hanging at my sides like nothing more than two anchors. It took everything I had to keep the serving tray from clattering to the floor.

The sounds made me think of blood red skies, vents of heat spilling their yellow sulfur, endless plains of white desolation, and the cold void of black stars. I wasn't sure why I thought these things, or why the images were so vivid, more than my best memories.

It was intrusive, strange, not my own…

"LEAH!"

Benny's voice cut through the fog, and I shook my head, the discordant symphony pushed aside. My bosses' eyes were hard, glancing between me and our customers, gesturing for me to come back to the kitchen.

It didn't feel right to walk away. My stomach rumbled and I felt cold, an odd sensation this time of year, even if it was nighttime. Benny quickly grabbed me when I stumbled through the door, putting his hand to my forehead and staring at me as I struggled in his grasp. "What the hell!?"

He put a finger to his lips and I immediately stopped struggling. He released his grip, and pointed back out to the dining room. My first instinct was to see where he was pointing, but something else seized me, a smell that was new, fascinating, delectable…

The fryers were operating at full blast, the sizzling grease was so loud it drowned out the radio outside. I found myself taking a step forward when Benny's fingers snapped in front of my face.

"Uh… what?" I asked, struggling with my words.

Benny's hands wrapped around my shoulders, and he guided me towards the order window. I heard his voice in my ear. "What are they doing?"

Harvey hadn't eaten his food; he was watching the radio, hands twitching. My eyes drifted to Cathy. She was slack-jawed, eyes closed like she was listening to a symphony.

I could see the four kids in the booth in the corner mirror. They had shifted in their seats to stare directly at the radio, their meal and coffee forgotten. Evan wasn't much better; he'd picked up one of the cheap red cups we used and held it in a shaking hand. His eyes were open wide, and his mouth was slightly open, not in wonder, but sudden understanding.

Over the fryers and the ever-present fan, I heard the sound reach a crescendo, warbles and beeps rising to a fever pitch that died out in a long musical tone that was familiar, but I couldn't quite place.

Then Harvey turned back to his food, the teenagers returned to their games, and Evan began to work on the table he'd been sent out to clean. I was confused, my mind trying to come up with any reasonable explanation.

What is happening? What are those sounds?

Benny's eyes jumped between each of them. I wanted to ask if this had happened before, but the frown on his face told me all I needed.

"Some radio contest, clues or something?" I whispered.

Benny looked at me and I realized how hollow the words sounded, but I didn't know what else it could be, what I could rationalize it as.

Cathy rose from her table and immediately walked to the door. Evan sat the box of dirty plates on the table and made a beeline for the alcove containing the incredibly small bathrooms.

A locked gaze with Benny told me that he was just as mystified as I was, then I saw Harvey rise from his seat. His face was peeling, red like a fresh coat of paint. He'd poured the coffee over his head. It was still dripping off his chin, staining the already-soiled white t-shirt with brown spots. He headed straight for the kitchen.

Benny spread his arm in front of me, staring our regular down. Harvey pushed through the double doors and shoved past the two of us, heading for the grease. He paused over it and looked at us.

It sent chills up my spine. Those eyes didn't register the pain he should have been feeling. They stared through the two of us, the head cocking slightly, and then he plunged both of his hands into the grease.

I felt the bile rise in the back of my throat. Benny reached a hand towards Harvey before thinking better of it. The smell hit us, dousing the kitchen with the odor of fried pig.

He looked at us one more time, and I knew. You could call it too many years serving food to all manner of people, or a gift of intuition, but I just had a feeling for people.

I didn't have a feeling for Harvey anymore, and what was behind those eyes wasn't human. He bared his teeth at us, whatever he was now trying to smile.

"Warm," he croaked.

I knew what he was going to do, and I screamed, "No!"

He plunged his face into the grease and began to spasm. I was frozen in place, but Benny didn't hesitate, rushing forward and trying to pull Harvey out.

"Leah! Help me!" Benny roared, snapping me out of my stupor, and I stumbled to help. I yelped when one of Harvey's hands splashed fresh grease from the vat onto my arm. I ran to the sink, fumbling with the tap and sighing when the cool breath of water came pouring.

I glanced back at Harvey. His hands were charred down to the bone, bits of raw muscle and broiled nerve curling to reveal the white knuckles. I could see the vein on his neck and the iron grip on the searing trap. For every inch that Benny won, Harvey gained two more.

Then he went slack and he slid further down. Benny grabbed him by the shirt and heaved. Harvey hit the floor and I heard a wet smacking as something red and aerated ran from his head.

Harvey's hair was charred and his face had peeled back to expose his skull, his skin running off onto the floor. I felt my knees give out as I struggled to hold in my dinner and failed.

Benny crouched next to me, patting my back, but he never stopped staring at Harvey. He leaned close when he saw that I was just trying to catch my breath. "Are you ok?"

I nodded, trying not to look at the man I'd spent nine years getting to know. "Why'd he do it?"

Benny stood glancing out of the order window. "You heard it, better than even me."

I must've looked like a deer in the headlights. Benny pursed his lips and then pointed a finger to the ceiling. "Out there, in the stars. We've spent decades pumping our noise, telling everything what we are."

He glanced at Harvey. "Only a matter of time before they start sending us the same."

My stomach clenched and my heart began to race. I didn't want to believe it, I would just rationalize this away too. The only things in this world were what we could see, touch, and feel.

Deny and rationalize, but I believed Benny. I'd seen the strange sky, the myriad suns burning close. I'd felt the needs and wants they'd sent us. They wanted us to know them, just like we'd sent our feelings out looking for the same. 24 hours a day there was always some transmission being flung off this little blue orb spinning in the black.

And something had picked them up.

"We've got to get to my car or your truck. Get into the city, or call the police, or…" I was rattling off solutions like they were the winning lotto numbers, but Benny shook his head. "You're half right. Get on the phone and call whoever you can think of, but keep your head down."

He stood up and headed towards his office while I scrambled to the breakroom opposite. My phone and purse were in a double locker that Benny had managed to nick from the Salton School public auction. I fumbled with the touch screen, joy leaping through me when I finally got it unlocked. Then came the all-important question of who I should ring in the middle of the night.

My parents and I were long on the outs, blessed months had passed since I had talked to them. Jessie was the only one who kept these hours, especially on a Friday. L.A.'s finest clubs would be open.

I pressed the CALL and waited, listening to my heart pounding with every ring. Finally, I heard a click as the call was picked up. "Oh, thank God, Jessie. I'm at the diner, we–"

There were clicks, odd beeping, and a low thrum of sounds that were nothing but consonants and hard rasps. I threw the phone away from me, trying not to listen to the sounds coming from it. My back hit the wall and I slid down until I found the floor. In the back of my mind, I knew that I had to turn it off, had to crawl over and expose my mind to whatever was riding the sound.

But I couldn't move.

Get up, get moving. You can still hear it, faint but it's there. How long can you bear it? Are you going to die in this diner? My thoughts ran like a runaway train, which I suppose was a blessing in a way. It meant that I was still human, still free of whatever was coming through my phone. The signal floating through the aether hadn't caught a hold of me.

I forced myself to crawl forward, humming to myself, trying to remember the old lullabies that I had grown up on. The screen on my phone was still lit, and I could see the red END CALL button like a target. I could hear the transmission coming through the speaker.

I fumbled with it, jabbing and trying not to listen to what was coming through the speaker, and finally I managed to disconnect the call.

Your name is Leah, you've worked here for nine years, you want to be an actress. My thoughts were like a mantra, reminding me of who I was. The phone was still in my hand, but I didn't dare dial again. I'd heard the sound twice; I didn't think it would be good to hear it a third time.

I jumped when I heard the footsteps and shrank back against the locker. There wasn't a weapon or anything that I could really use to defend myself if it came to it.

Could whatever had been playing through Harvey's mind get him back on his feet? How much skin and nerves did it need to pilot his corpse around? I closed my eyes. I didn't want to see his broiled face and mouth speaking about how warm his death had been.

"Leah?"

Benny.

I opened my eyes and saw the cook standing in the breakroom entry, a pistol clutched in his left hand, looking between me and the phone. "You good?"

I shook my head and held out the phone to him like he could suddenly fix it. He understood immediately, hefting the pistol into a shooter's grip and waving me to get behind him. I took my place, and he gestured with his head towards the knife rack, all manner of sizes and models resting easy in their berths.

"We're getting Evan and we're making for my house. We can work out a plan after." Benny said it with all the confidence of a man who had been here before, accustomed to danger. He had never been chatty about his past, always deflecting when I brought up a joke or a slightly prying question, but whatever he had been, I was grateful for it now.

He could wrap his mind and will around the unknown better than a D-list actress who could quote diner lingo like it was her second language. If Evan was in his right mind, he should thank his lucky stars. I would have left him behind.

I grabbed the biggest knife from the rack.

We paused when we reached the double doors to the dining hall. Benny glanced out, barely letting his eye be seen through the glass.

"Where are they?" I whispered.

Benny held up one finger. "I can see Cathy out of the window. She's tearing up her rig."

Faintly, I thought that I could hear it, the sounds of metal being thrown in the dirt. "What about those four assholes?"

Benny shook his head. "They're gone. Now stay close." He pushed through the doors, and we moved quickly. I glanced out of the window and saw Cathy's truck. She was tearing into the engine block, crouched in the machinery like some sort of animal cleaning its nest.

The restroom doors were to our left past the bar and the statue of Elvis that had consistently degraded with every season. The paint on his cheeks had peeled, so had his pompadour, but he loyally kept his post as guardsmen of the MEN and WOMEN'S room.

Benny crept forward to the Men's room, pausing against the door. I looked back at the empty diner, feeling my flesh crawl. The entry door was open slightly, each gust of wind caused it to rattle against the frame.

I could smell the coffee where I'd left it, and something else that had cooked too long. The booths were empty, the plates left dirty, our inhouse flies already descending to have their way with the leftovers.

For such a small building, it didn't feel empty.

Benny whispered my name, and I reluctantly turned my back on the place, joining him at the door. The little blue man waved at me from the MEN sign. Benny pressed his ear to the right of it and pulled me close. "Can you hear it?"

Gooseflesh prickled and I fumbled to readjust my knife as I pressed my own ear opposite him. It was quiet. I believed that Benny had heard *something* but I'd spent years blasting hair metal down I-95.

Then I heard the scratching.

It was faint, but furious, with pauses coming between each wave.

My stomach dropped when I realized it was mimicking the beats of the sound that had come through the radio. Benny pointed to my knife, an unspoken gesture to get ready. Then he pushed through the door.

Evan had torn off most of his clothes, a tattered pair of boxers the only thing still clinging to his frame. He was sweating profusely, every pore seemed like it was open and leaking. Through the sweat-stained mop of hair, I could see his eyes were fixed on his work. He'd torn off his nails scratching at the stalls, but that just meant he'd continued with his blood. He'd used every available surface as a canvas, creating symbols that hurt my eyes to see, swirling and jagged icons whose meaning was lost on me. It could have been some sort of code for all I knew.

I couldn't tell if Evan hadn't noticed us, or just didn't care, but he never paused from writing the otherworldly iconography. Benny kept the gun leveled at him when he whispered, "Evan?"

Evan paused for a moment, his hands trembling, then calmly wrote the next irregular symbol. Had he heard us? Was Evan still in there? I imagined him struggling through a deep well, trying to claw his way up and back out into the light.

Benny sighed, and raised the pistol, burying it into Evan's wet hair. I didn't know what to do, didn't want to watch, and I also knew that there wasn't anything else we could do.

Whatever Evan had written in here wasn't something anyone needed to know.

Evan turned when he felt the barrel. His eyes stared past us, through us. I had a feeling he was seeing the fault lines between worlds. Then he spoke, and his words washed over the both of us as sensations, images, intent conveyed through seized flesh. The vast and unknown heavens opened up to Benny and me, and I wanted to scream with what we saw.

I heard the gunshot and Evan's brains splattered over his manifesto. The deep maroon matter shimmered as fluorescent light reflected the neon green that was slowly spreading through his blood.

Benny looked over at me, two tears streaming down his cheeks. He pulled the hammer back on the pistol, and for a second, I thought he might kill me.

We knew now, there was no going back from that, we KNEW what was out there riding the vapor trails of comets and hiding in the silent darkness of asteroids. There was no more wonder, we had been told.

"Don't leave me," I whispered, wiping the tears from my cheek. "Please."

Benny hesitated, biting his lip. "There aren't any more questions. All that's left is what's on the other side."

His hand closed around the pistol grip and he sighed. "You still want to try? Want to keep living on this planet that doesn't know? You heard him… you heard *them.*"

Never thought I'd be doing this for thirty years.

Call it determination, knowing what I knew, or the idea that I didn't want to believe it was all meaningless, that the madness out in the sky had just given us a small snippet. I wanted to believe it was worth it.

"Yeah… God help me, but I do."

Benny stared at me, then at our dead friend, and finally the ceiling. The intent Evan had given was clear and I wondered which piece of fear Benny was working through, all the possibilities of what could happen next and if he was willing to weather them. He turned and opened the door. "Come on, we've got more to put out of their misery."

The smell of grease was gone when we came back out. A menagerie of techno-organic matter was growing across the walls. They pulsed in otherworldly light. I smelled rotten eggs and looked at Benny who took one whiff and whispered, "Sulfur." The conduits were growing from Harvey's corpse; I knew it as intrinsically as I knew how to breathe, and they'd found their desired customers.

Four figures crouched around just as many shoots, the ends shoved into their mouths, taking deep breaths. Foam was spilling out with each breath, vomit spilling between their lips as they spasmed. Their eyes were glazed over, uncaring that each breath was killing them. One was sprawled on his stomach, occasionally twitching as he desperately took another breath. The girl was slumped against a booth, her hands wrapped around the conduit that grew out of the neon mass.

The last two seemed to be in a competition to see who could last the longest. They were on their knees, each haggard breath sending fresh waves of vomit splattering onto the floor. The intelligences that had taken root craved the poison they were inhaling and didn't care that its piloted flesh was dying with every breath.

The guilt gnawed at me, every bad thought that I'd had for them playing again, and each one falling short as I watched the kid furthest from me topple forward, a bloody slosh spilling out of his mouth.

Benny didn't hesitate; there were three quick shots to the ones that were incapacitated, more of the glowing blood peppering our tables, then we came to the last. He was on his knees, one hand balled in a fist keeping him upright, the other keeping a rigid grip on the tube. Benny took a small breath and pressed the gun against the back of his head.

He wrapped his finger around the trigger, but he didn't fire. There was another noise, a low thrumming that seemed to beat in my chest, a sound like an engine revving up.

Cathy was standing in the doorway. Her pupils had grown like dinner plates, two portals to the outer dark lodged in her sockets. Her skin was transparent; I could see the veins pumping the green phosphorescence through the high-octane valves of her new mechanical heart. Her body and her truck had become one, a union made by the stars.

The sound was coming from her right hand. It glowed the same sickly green, the machinery intertwined with her bones flooding an opening in her hand the size of the dinner plate with the same glow…

When she fired it sounded like a broken fanbelt and the emerald lance struck like lightning. Benny dived, tackling me out of the way. The two of us landed in the tangle of tubing and alien detritus.

The green light hit the kid and I watched the layers of his flesh flay off like someone had pressed fast forward. His skin peeled and burned, then his muscles, and finally his organs, all in the blink of an eye. All that was left was a skeleton, one that was already warping to resemble something else.

Benny shoved himself to a knee, firing three shots at Cathy. The bullets found their marks, and she staggered but all it did was draw the otherworldly blood. Cathy jabbed the weapon embedded in her arm forward and another ray of light fired.

I'd closed my eyes assuming I'd open them in front of the pearly gates. Instead, I heard Benny screaming. The ray had caught him in the arm, the pistol and bullets had instantly melted into a glob of burning metal that soaked the stub of where his arm would be. It had burned and unraveled in the green fire.

Cathy staggered forward, the alien weapon in her arm was growing, it was nearly longer than her leg, and she struggled to move and aim it properly. That was the only thing that saved us. Before this, I never would have thought I could have dragged Benny anywhere, but somehow, I hauled him through the kitchen doors, crying and begging him to stand up.

Whatever *they* had downloaded into Harvey, it had taken root. Machinery pumped out plumes of sulfur, things that could have been eggs or plants beat in unnatural undulations, pulsing with unearthly colors. I struggled to breathe as the gas burned the back of my throat.

Benny waved his spare hand, coughing, determined eyes fixed on me. "Go out the back, get out, and make it matter."

There was no argument. I nodded and left him lying on the floor. The sulfur was stinging his eyes. He waved a hand again to clear the air, coughing. "Gas… unplug the gas line…" He devolved into a coughing fit, falling back on the floor and dry heaving. From out in the diner, I heard the whirring gears and the hard speech coming from the thing that used to be Cathy.

In a daze, I followed Benny's instructions, then was racing out the back and into the dry night air. My car sat like it didn't have a care in the world and I fumbled with my keys, nearly breaking out in song when the unlock chime beeped.

I keyed the ignition and put the JUNIPER FLAVOR DINER in my rearview. A quarter mile down the road, I saw a faint green flash and then the entire building went up in a tower of orange fire.

The explosion rocked the car, causing me to swerve across the asphalt, weaving back and forth until I finally managed to get myself back under control. The tears came freely, and I rested my head on the wheel, watching the orange glow consume a footprint of my life and the sounds that had come down from the sky.

The radio kicked on in my car and a small crackle of static came through the dial, followed by a sound… faint, but getting louder.

It was a familiar tune.

Mochés
Robert Essig

Chef Fontaine couldn't believe it. He'd managed to create yet another astonishing dish that had taken the culinary world by storm. Food Magazine was scheduled for an interview and photo shoot next week. It wasn't exactly the caviar of food literature, but Fontaine wasn't picky on his rise to fine dining fame. Every article, every exposé, every television interview was a brick in the wall of total culinary domination.

On this night his new signature dish, mochés, was being consumed by famous San Diego food critic Horatio Stevenson. Horatio wrote for such exquisite local fares as *Fine Dining in San Diego*, *North County Living*, and *La Jolla Lifestyles*. His articles were often published in national magazines such as *Wine and Country*, *Rich Life*, and *Troubadour*. Not to mention his local reviews were often reprinted in the New York Times and other major publications across the country.

Horatio Stevenson was a big deal. Chef Fontaine knew him well. Horatio had critiqued many a dish, always giving rave reviews, which, if Fontaine's head wasn't so big, he couldn't deny as being one of the driving forces to his notoriety.

Fontaine only greeted his most esteemed customers with a special appetizer when he thought he could get something out of them. Politicians, dignitaries, filthy rich activists, that sort of person. Horatio was no exception. And the appetizer was the dish he was there to critique.

"Chef Fontaine," Horatio said, "so great to see you again."

Fontaine approached the table with a bowl in hand and a smile that was only vaguely removed from a condescending smirk. This was all show. Fontaine didn't give a damn about Horatio as a person. All he wanted was a good review. Perhaps Mochés would be the dish that catapulted is fame worldwide.

"So great to see you, Horatio," Fontaine said as he stopped at the table, cradling the bowl. "What I have for you today is a dish that will send your senses into uncharted plateaus of ecstasy."

A server saddled up to Fontaine carrying a stainless steel gravy boat held in a pristine white cloth.

Fontaine placed the dish before Horatio. He looked into the critic's eyes, trying to read his first response, but Horatio was a stoic man who kept his observations to himself. Outside of the smile greeting, he was all business and would remain so for the rest his evening in Fontaine's five star restaurant, never once giving even the slightest hint of whether he enjoyed a dish or not. Fontaine always watched him closely, hoping for a glimpse of emotion to indicate what could be expected in the write up, but Horatio was a master of keeping himself in check at all times while sampling a dish he was to critique.

Horatio looked up at Fontaine, but said nothing. His eyes indicated that he wanted an explanation, but it was as if he feared verbally expressing such a thing would reveal too much of his first impressions.

"I present you Mochés," Fontaine said.

In the bowl was a writhing of large worms that resembled maggots, each one speckled with tiny red measles-like dots. The twisted and turned and slithered amongst one another, their little heads with beady black eyes popping up and telescoping around as if to see something other than the stark white of the deep dish in which they'd been served.

Fontaine registered a hint of caution from Horatio.

"Please allow Geraldo to pour the broth over them. It is at a temperature that will begin to cook the Mochés, but I suggested you begin eating them while they cook, for the full experience." As Geraldo slowly poured the hot broth over the worms, steam rising from the bowl to release a pleasant fragrance, Fontaine continued introducing the dish. "The Mochés are cultivated locally. They are fed on a specific diet that creates a unique flavor you will only find in this dish." Fontaine nodded. "Bon apetít!"

Amore A Mochés by Horatio Stevenson

I am no new comer to downtown hot spot Soleil and ingenious owner chef Fontaine. I have said of Fontaine that he has the culinary skills of an acrobat walking a tight rope over a bed of rusty nails, always moving forward and never looking down. I am quite certain that chef Fontaine is the future of food in not only America, but the entire world. My latest foray into his prodigious world of flavor was no exception.

One exquisite dish can change a man's life. Can change a man's perspective. Mochés is that dish. The translation is, well, non-existent, as it seems chef Fontaine is pretentious enough to invent his own words. In this case, he has every right to do so, for he has created a dish that should be served to the gods themselves. A dish so breathtaking and original in its renderings that world leaders and jet setting socialites alike will be flocking to Soleil as a culinary destination for years to come, solely to sample chef Fontaine's mochés.

Mochés is a dish served fresh from a source Fontaine keeps secret, but I am assured is local. Perhaps mochés are sea worms? Don't let that lithe image deter you from the sheer brilliance of this dish. The mochés are served live in a bowl over which is ladled the most aromatic broth I have encountered in years. The temperature is scalding, which begins to cook the mochés before the patron's eyes in a flash of display that is pleasing to all senses. The mochés writhe and squirm as the succulent broth cooks them to perfection.

I was admittedly apprehensive about eating what looked like grubs, but I am a consummate professional who never turns down a dish however unusual it may appear. I took in a sampling of the mochés, savoring the aromatic broth, the little grub wiggling around my mouth, which added something unexpected via full use of the senses. When I bit down it popped in a glorious display of flavor that complimented the broth in ways I was not fully prepared for. Hints of a deep blue cheese pungency met with the aroma of the sea, melding with the delectable broth like infused butter. The creaminess of the mochés creates a texture like the most decadent cream sauce that explodes with savory notes of sea life yet undiscovered, cheeses reserved for those with the most adventurous and extraordinary palates, all blended together in glorious harmony.

Mochés is a dish you won't soon forget. A dish that will be the talk of the town. An experience like no other, this will be an acquired taste for the mere layman, but a sensuous and lingering engagement for those who take fine dining as seriously as I do.

***

Fontaine, beaming from Horatio's rave review of mochés in *San Diego Fine Dining*, opened the door to the storage basement. The lights were on, indicating that his sous chefs were busy harvesting mochés for tonight's appetizers.

As Fontaine descended the old wooden steps, the smell of the cellar smacked him in the face, and though he was prepared for it, the smell caused him to grimace every time. He used to get queasy and once even vomited, but he'd become somewhat accustomed to it. Somewhat. His sous chefs had stronger stomachs than he. They had to or he'd fire them. They also wore masks while they worked.

At the bottom of the steps Fontaine took in the rank ambiance of the place with newfound valor and appreciation. He'd often pondered where the limitations of food actually were, speculating that with enough finesse, anything could be made palatable. He took that mode of thinking and considered it a challenge, and with mochés, he'd reached new heights.

"You here to get some moochies for yourself?" a hoarse voice said.

Chef Fontaine glared at the woman who spoke. She was the only one who ever spoke to him. She stared at him now like she had the day they met, out back in the alley while Fontaine was on a cigarette break. She'd come up to him out of nowhere, dirty hair in a stringy mess, face etched with deep craters like a fleshy moonscape. She was twitchy, eyes like listless caves. Fontaine had ignored her, but she was insistent, mumbling about her moochies.

Seeing her in the cage with the others caused the rancid smell of the basement storage room to become that much more stifling. It was these women who smelled so bad, locked here and deprived of so much as a shower. Clean bodies didn't produce mochés.

Extracting the mochés was a two-man job and had to be done every morning to ensure there was enough for the dinner rush later that evening. RJ was hunched over one of the nameless crack whores. She'd been knocked out. She'll be disappointed to wake up and find she's still alive. Twiggy worked next to him, his tall and lean frame hunched over a bowl, performing the first act of preparing the mochés for consumption.

"You never did try my moochies, did you?" the woman said, her voice rough and sort of far away.

She'd spoken of moochies that day she pestered Fontaine in the alley. He tried to ignore her, but she'd been insistent, as cracked-out individuals can be. She was higher than a jet airliner, pupils like pinpricks, as she held out her hand. Fontaine was going to put his cigarette out in her cupped palm, just to make a statement, but then he saw the worms. She held a small pile of writhing worms like he'd never seen before. They were like large maggots, only they had hairs on them. Fontaine had never seen anything like it. He was repulsed, about to swat the offering away and tell the woman to get the hell away from his establishment before he called the police, but then he got an idea. His most hated critic had been dining there that night. The man was an insufferable prick. Fontaine knew the only reason Gibson Belview critiqued his dishes was to give him bad press.

That was the day it all started.

Half the basement had been fitted with large cages that contained ten cracked-out junkie bitches. Fontaine had no bleeding heart for such degenerates. They'd paved their road in life and they were walking it. He kept them high on crack and heroin, which was cheap and easy to acquire. They kept him in mochés. Most of them were leaned against the wall, strung out. The mochés that skittered along the floor were the easy ones to get, but extraction was necessary to ensure enough product each evening.

The woman stood at the bars of the cage and stared at Fontaine while one hand was between her grime-smeared legs, fingers deep in the cleft of her vagina. Fontaine grimaced. A smell seemed to reach out from the messy vortex of her womanhood and threaten a violent vomitary reaction. She withdrew her hand and offered up her goods.

"Fresh from the source," she said, eyes wild with insanity. Her smile displayed brown teeth, gapped where they'd fallen out as a result of her dopetooth. Fontaine was surprised she didn't have bugs in her gums.

The worms writhed in her hand, just like the day she weaseled her way into Fontaine's life. Fat maggots with coarse hairs, glistening with her rotten fish smelling secretions.

Fontaine turned away, approaching his faithful workers. RJ reared back from the knocked-out crack whore in the stirrups. He sighed. "It doesn't get any easier to do this."

Fontaine looked down at the woman, her legs spread like she were about to get a gynecological exam. Below her was a bowl of wiggling hairy maggots.

"Oop, there's one," Fontaine said.

RJ extended his gloved hand to pluck a maggot from the gaping mouth of the gangrenous vagina, but it seemed to sense he was coming for it, and it withdrew back inside of her.

"I think she's done," he said. "For today."

RJ passed the bowl to Twiggy, who painstakingly used a gentle grip with rubber coated tweezers to hold the worms while carefully extracting each thick, curly hair, which resulted in a small red dot, giving the worms an exotic appearance that seemed to compliment their final duty as the most extraordinary appetizer in five-star dining.

Fontaine grabbed a bowl of plucked worms and pondered on how desperate people had to be to attempt eating moldy cheeses, nasty looking fungus, spiny creatures from the depths of the sea, or even eggs that had been buried and rotting. Intestines, fish so foul it gave off an ammonia reek. Desperate times that created dishes people cherished to this day.

And to think, a bastard of a critic ate these pussy maggots and wrote a rave review about a most foul dish, hoping it would destroy a good chef, only to have his bad intentions backfire and create a culinary god.

Unfound Footage
Patrick Lacey

I found the skull half buried on a path in Cat Town. It was hard work pushing aside the damp soil and I earned myself a slice on my index finger, one that bled until I wrapped it with paper towels and packing tape.

I was low on Band-Aids.

And also money.

I'd traveled to Cat Town to location scout for the film. Uncle Harold had agreed to help finance the project. Harold was a dentist with one foot in the retirement community and too much money in his pockets. His accountant suggested he put some of that money somewhere other than his bank account. He cut me a check for ten grand. Not exactly Hollywood dough but more than enough for what we had planned.

The skull was almost loose after twenty minutes. I twisted and pulled and something gave. I wonder if there's still a neck-down skeleton under there. It's amazing, the secrets you walk over each day, on your way to school or work, if either of those are your bag.

What struck me most was the pearl white of the bone, like the grime and worms had no interest in clinging to its contours. I hadn't been this close to a skull since high school biology but from what I remembered, between hits of my vaporizer in the bathroom, most weren't this big.

And most didn't have horns.

At least that's what they looked like. Two bony protrusions pushing out of where the hair must have been. It resembled a Halloween decoration, a prop you purchased for too much money at a pop-up shop in late September. But those skulls weren't this heavy and the horns were usually curled like those of a ram. These were small and part of the bone structure.

It would be perfect set dressing.

I forgot to mention: we were making a *horror* movie.

I carried the skull with me while I scoped out Cat Town.

You may be wondering: why the name?

Most folks say it's because of the stray feline community that populates the zigging and zagging paths. What you don't hear, though, is how those cats got there in the first place. Many years prior, when being called a witch still got you mob justice, there was a leper colony out there. Banished from the town because of their skin lesions. Some said it was the devil's mark, that the lepers had been consorting with the dark lord outside the fire's light.

It was probably something contagious, not supernatural, though these days I think the holy crowd was on to something.

I assumed the skin condition accounted for the horns and abnormal girth. I'd found one of the original colony members. The thing belonged in a local museum, not our low budget found footage film. Maybe after we wrapped, I could find a curator nearby and cut him a good deal.

I kept to the outer paths. They were easier to navigate. Cat Town was something of a spiral with its branching paths. The closer you got to its center, the harder it was to find your way back. The colony's shacks had been reduced to piles of brick and stone. We could build them up if need be. I wasn't worried about permits, about disturbing Cat Town. Forest rangers found better things to do with their time, kept the public parks pristine when this place was overgrown with brush. Even the beware-of-tick signs were hidden behind vines.

I took photos of the rocks with strange symbols and words from languages you won't find in any college textbook. Like I would know. Most of it was probably mumbo-jumbo, scrawls from the colony as leprosy boiled their brains. But some of it made a strange sort of sense, like if I squinted the translation would come together.

The shadows grew longer. I checked my watch. Going on four. I'd arrived early that morning—early for me at least—to allow plenty of time before dusk. But dusk, it would seem, was already intruding. Last I'd checked, it was noon, which meant what felt like an hour was more like four. I chocked it up to nerves. I had to admit: being in Cat Town alone was enough to keep me on edge.

I looked at the winding paths in either direction but neither seemed familiar. I'd taken note of the markers along the way but couldn't spot them now, not with the way the sun was sinking. It would be dark soon. It was October and night came quickly.

My phone rang.

I held my chest and answered. "Yeah?"

"Been trying to reach you for an hour." Anthony. Annoyed, like the bad service was my fault, but I checked my screen. Four bars. Zero calls and just as many voicemail messages.

"Hunter, you there?"

I shook my head. My thoughts were sticky like tar. "This place is perfect," I said. "It'll need some tinkering but we can make it looked haunted no problem."

"I talked to Lexi and she's game. So is Brad."

"Nice," I said, noticing that the trees stood still. Not a single leaf fell from their branches, though I felt the breeze on my skin.

Brad was a decent actor, had graduated from high school plays to community theater. He might ham it up for the camera but that wasn't such a bad thing. And Lexi rarely wore a bra. Our film was coming together, yet I couldn't be bothered with excitement.

"Earth to Brad."

"That all sounds good. Listen, I'll see you tomorrow. Show you around the place. Give you the proper tour."

Anthony kept talking but I ended the call. I studied the way the breeze blew through the path but didn't disturb the trees. I plucked the closest leaf from its branch. It came loose with little effort and crumbled to dust in my palm. I backed away, onto the path, and chose the direction that felt most like an exit. The sky was turning the color of bruises when I found the parking lot and my beat-to-shit Honda.

The engine rolled over a few times, like Cat Town didn't want me to leave. I pulled out of the lot and drove for three miles before I remembered the skull.

I'd been cradling it, like a sleeping infant.

That night, like all nights, I got high and watched horror movies.

My finger was red beneath the tape. I could've borrowed a Band-Aid from my sister but that would've further proved her point that I was broke and incapable of living alone. I *could* live that way if I hadn't burned through my inheritance. Mom and Dad left us twenty grand each after the funeral costs. Sis bought the house, let me stay in her finished basement while she raised a family above. I bought the flat-screen TV, sound bar, and five hundred and thirty-two horror movies. Mostly Blu-rays but also some DVDs and VHS tapes for good measure. I watched everything. Good, bad, garbage. I had become somewhat of an expert of the genre these last few years, which is how I met a producer from Screamatorium Pictures.

Alec frequented the same message boards. We often engaged in heated disputes over which *Wishmaster* sequel was better. We kept in touch. I performed the occasional odd job for him, edited YouTube videos on the fly, learning the craft as I went.

Two months before Cat Town, we'd been chatting over messenger. Alec mentioned wanting to produce a found footage film. He had some extra money from the prior summer's convention circuit and since the format tended to run cheap, he figured it was a safe investment.

Enter me.

I pitched him on the spot. The same story that's been told for forty years now. A bunch of kids in the woods find something bad waiting for them. Good thing he wasn't looking for quality. Screamatorium got their films distributed to Wal-Mart clearance bins and people, whoever they were, bought them. He didn't sound impressed until I mentioned Cat Town.

"*The* Cat Town?" he asked, being somewhat of a paranormal enthusiast.

"The one and only," I said, knowing I had him.

And now, two months later, that wasn't all I had.

I'd propped the skull on the windowsill. I could see its reflection on the television screen, which didn't seem possible. The sun was well past set and the lack of light should've cast no reflections. But it was there, in the upper right corner, each time the screen faded to black.

Above, I could hear Sis putting Teddy and Jocelyn to bed. Irish twins even if Sis insisted they were both planned. She also insisted I was a textbook example of "failure to launch." What she didn't know was I had no *desire* to launch. I was content in the basement. Careers and families took effort and effort I did not have.

The film ended, the credits splashing the basement in shadows.

The skull was there, in the same corner.

I tossed in another disc at random and began to doze. The lines played through my dreams. At some point, they transitioned to wordless whispers. I woke with a start, certain that Sis had come down to lower the volume but I was alone. Looking toward the window, I saw the skull was in the same position, yet it felt disturbed somehow. It was the feeling of walking into a room, certain only moments before, the space had been occupied.

The radiator hummed and hissed, which accounted for what had sounded like voices moments before. Sweat soaked my shirt and my skin itched, dry patches along my arms I blamed on being outside in the chill air for too long.

I tried sleeping again. Each time I nodded off, I remembered the skull. Each time I checked, it remained static. We continued this dance until the sun painted the sky orange.

"What's my motivation?" Brad asked for the dozenth time.

"Act scared," I said, coughing out smoke from my lungs.

We'd built a fire and were eating a dinner of burnt hot dogs and s'mores. Earlier that day, we'd gone over the "script," using the term lightly. I'd written the bullet-point version of the story but decided to give the talent the liberty of improvising. That's how they'd done it in *The Blair Witch Project*, and they'd become millionaires in the process. Granted, I was getting paid in experience but Alec promised me top billing. My name above the title, whatever the title would be.

"I need more than that," Brad said, reading his pages by the light of the fire. His greasy fingertips left smears on the paper.

Lexi rolled her eyes and asked me to pass the joint. She was a woman of few words, which worked for the script since she'd mostly be screaming. I tried to remain professional, to focus on her eyes. She'd been my crush all through junior and senior year, just high enough on the social ladder to be unobtainable. Time had not changed that. Still, when we managed something like conversation, she was filled with insight. For some reason, she didn't want people thinking she was smart. I liked knowing her secret.

Something moved in the brush behind us. The shadow was tall and thin and I was glad to see it was just Anthony, returning from his piss in the woods. Higher and drunker than the rest of us, he stumbled, used the trees for balance.

"You scared the shit out of me," I said, turning back to the fire.

"Who were you expecting?" he said, going for his second hot dog.

I didn't answer him.

A few minutes' walk down the path was the shack we'd built up that week. It didn't look much like the original, at least not according to the renditions I'd found online, but the darkness would hide most of the flaws. Besides, whoever picked up our disc from the bargain bin probably wasn't concerned with historical accuracy. We'd set-dressed the interior with a stack of bibles purchased from a church sale. The old woman at the register was impressed with our wanting to study scripture. She didn't know about the latex binding we'd crafted to resemble human skin. Anthony had carved a pentagram into the floor, tossed in a few candles.

In the middle, of course, lay the skull.

I'd sprinkled some salt around it, told Anthony it was something real witches did. But really I was documenting any movement.

"I don't get it," Brad said. "Why would we be in the woods this late anyway? We're supposed to college students—*grad* students—writing a paper about occult activity. We're, what, mid to late twenties? Shouldn't we know better? We'd stick to daylight. We'd come prepared."

"Sounds like someone's never seen a horror movie," Lexi said.

"I've seen plenty," Brad said.

"Name one."

"The hockey masked one, where he kills people in their dreams."

"Jesus," Lexi said between puffs. "This is going to be a long night."

All around us, the forest swam with movement. Twigs snapping. Leaves crunching. The felines of Cat Town stuck to the shadows, wary of strangers. I found it odd not one stray had stepped toward the light and the promise of a warm meal. It took some getting used to, the constant chatter of Cat Town's wildlife, but eventually it faded to background noise, like crickets or distant traffic.

As the group gathered the equipment, I stared into the darkness. The moon was full but it didn't stretch past the trees. Outside of the fire's flickering, it was the kind of dark you couldn't find in the city or the suburbs, the kind not polluted by streetlights or porch lamps.

The kind that's been there from the beginning.

"Something got you spooked?" Lexi said, planting a hand on my shoulder.

My heart sped then slowed. Out here, there wasn't time for hormones. Besides, it was just a friendly touch.

I shrugged. "This place has quite the history."

"So you said." This close, her breath smelled like hot dogs and weed and whatever fruity lip gloss she'd applied. "But that was hundreds of years ago. Leprosy is gone and so are the lepers. The most we're going to find tonight is a couple of hungry kitties. And don't worry, I've got us covered." From her purse, she revealed a plastic bag of cat

106

treats. Salmon flavored. She pulled out a handful of tiny pink morsels. "Hungry?"

I let out something like a laugh. "Still full from dinner. Thanks, though."

"Suit yourself." She tossed several of the treats into the shadows. "Here, kitty kitty."

We heard them scattering, heard them pounce and chew, but the strange thing was how they didn't beg for more, didn't offer a single famished meow or thankful purr.

"For strays," Lexi said, "they sure are polite."

"This place stinks," Brad said of our makeshift shack.

He was on to something. The place had grown rancid since that afternoon. It smelled of decay, of food left to rot. Maybe something had used the structure as a shelter, had itself a night-time snack before moving on.

The candles still burned. Their flames appeared to be in the same positions. The wax had not melted any further.

And yes, the skull remained inside the circle of salt.

"Let's go over it one last time," I said as we huddled.

Lexi and Brad groaned. They weren't writing this off as a passion project but they weren't taking it too seriously either. They understood the potential, how if we got enough eyes on the film, it could open doors for all of us. More roles for them, more directing opportunities for me. Assuming I figured out how to direct this time around. Anthony seemed neither annoyed nor ecstatic. For him, this was just another Friday night. He had some experience with movies, had attended one and a half semesters of film school before dropping out to work the front desk at a boutique video rental shop. He'd be assisting with the gags, throwing stones against the shack, snapping twigs to add to the ambience.

The plan was to let Lexi and Brad do their thing, hold the cameras as our grad student characters would. Anthony would remain just outside the shack to mess with them and

I'd stay further back, watching all three. If something wasn't working, I'd let them know. If they fumbled what little lines were written in the script, I'd let them know.

And if we needed to get out of there in a hurry, I'd let them know.

"We good?" I said after the spiel.

"You're sure we wouldn't call the cops first?" Brad said. "Before we came out here alone?"

Lexi rubbed her eyes, as red and bloodshot as mine felt. "You see the one with the possessed girl from Haddonfield?" she said.

Brad kept quiet and read the greasy script one last time.

"I'll give it to you," Anthony said on our way out. "The skull looks great. Where'd you say you bought it again?"

"A guy on Craigslist," I said too fast, like the skull might answer for me. I wasn't sure why I'd lied, why I couldn't admit to finding it poking from the soil.

I'm still not.

Outside the shack, Anthony snapped a branch in half

"You hear that?" Lexi said. Her name was Leslie in the script. Not much of stretch and neither was her character. True, she hadn't gone to grad school, but aside from a few throwaway lines about her thesis project on occult activities, Leslie was Lexi and vice versa.

Brad, though—Brad leaned so far into his character he just might topple over. He played Brock like this wasn't a cheap cash-in but a Broadway musical. I wanted to yell *cut*, have them take it from the top, but they were too deep into the scene now. I'd see how things played out.

"I've heard *plenty* of things," Brad/Brock said. "It doesn't feel safe here. It feels like we're being watched from every angle and any minute, whatever's watching is going to pounce."

I nodded from the tree line.

Not bad.

Anthony went around the other side of the shack to scratch his fingernails along the wood. The sound echoed in the night. We could manipulate it in post, make it seem guttural. Not that it needed much altering. This far from the group, standing alone in the dark, it wasn't difficult to imagine the sound had come from behind instead of ahead.

"Jesus," Lexi/Leslie said, "what if those lepers never died out?" A pause for dramatic effect. "What if they've come back?"

Something shifted in the air. My ears gave out for a moment, then sound began to fade back in. I blamed it on earwax, on too much weed and not enough sleep. I wondered if the others felt it too.

"I find it hard to believe," Brad/Brock said, his voice different now, like he'd had an epiphany, like his character was calling the shots, "that they remained unnoticed for so long. Hikers, joggers—someone must have run into them along the way. But maybe what they saw was so terrible, so beyond the scope of what their brains could interpret, they dropped dead on the spot or maybe they ran home to their families and tried to keep it a secret. Tried but *failed*. Because when they slept that night and all the nights after, what they saw was skin, diseased and tumorous, and how there seemed to be a terrible pattern to the lesions, not unlike the markings on the rocks, and the more they tried to think of happy things like vacations and playground dates, the more that pattern unfolded so that thinking of *anything* else became impossible and they found themselves wandering back here, back to Cat Town. And here they'll stay."

I stood in awe at the improvised lines. They seemed at once unnatural and on the money. Far from realistic yet the dialogue made the scene more surreal.

I scratched my arms.

Not bad at all.

"Has it crossed your mind even once," Brad/Brock went on, "that maybe the villagers were right to condemn the lepers, that they were on to something with their dark arts theory? Only it wasn't as simple as casting spells and chanting in the woods. There are worse things out there than witches, worse even than the devil. There are places so dark and pitiful, imagining them would cause your blood to simmer out your ears and your eyes would burst from the pressure."

He continued on. Someone had done their research. He seemed to know all about the history of this place. But he knew other things too. Things he couldn't have read in any textbook.

I opened my mouth to end the scene. Brad was drifting too far into left field.

That's when the door slammed shut.

At first I thought Anthony had rigged it with a rope, except he was still on the far side of the shack.

"Hey," Lexi said from inside, her voice muffled now. "This isn't in the script."

"Will you shut your filthy mouth?" Brad said, only now he was mostly Brock. "Have you not been listening? You are not in Cat Town. It doesn't work that way. Cat Town is in you."

"What's that smell?" Lexi said, sniffing and gagging.

Before I could blame it on the original scent, the rotten air I'd been unable to pinpoint, I smelled it too.

It wasn't carrion this time.

Something was burning.

"Jesus," Lexi said between sharp inhales, "this isn't funny."

I called for Anthony but he didn't answer. I jogged across the path and tried to push the door open. The wood was littered with splinters, tiny slivers lodging into my palms. It had been cheap but not dry and jagged. These were not the same two-by-fours we'd stolen from the

110

lumberyard. These appeared, somehow, to be much older. The shack was hot to the touch, like the flames had spread. Black smoke seeped from between the gaps. I asked Lexi and Brock—sorry, Brad—if they were okay but Lexi had grown silent and Brad wouldn't shut up.

"They say dogs are man's best friend but they couldn't be more wrong. Dogs are blindly loyal to their owners. You can feed a dog the same gruel each day and then, without warning, you can cage and famish them and yet, before they finally grow rabid, finally regress to the beasts they were meant to be, they'll cling to the hope that their mush you call food will be presented to them, that they can put this bad business in the past. Cats, though—cats are indifferent. You know, if you dropped dead this instant, your cat would only wait a full day before feasting on you? They'd start with the eyes of course, for they are accessible and tender." His voice had lowered by octaves and he'd developed something of an accent, vaguely British yet not quite. Brad was a decent actor but he'd never been this convincing.

I rounded the structure and found no sign of Anthony. The brush shook but nothing stepped forward. I called to him twice and received no answer save for the cats just out of sight.

"Lexi," I said, pummeling the back of the shack, cursing us for not installing a window. "Lexi, if you can hear me, you need to break down the door from the inside."

Brad's voice was growing deeper by the word. "…and skin was made to be filthy with rot and scars and disease and we are meant to wither with time so that we may look more like that which will *not* cast us out, that which will *accept* us into its mangled arms and caress us with fingernails long like talons. Beauty is cancer. Suffering, sickness—*those* are the true miracles."

I found a gap larger than the rest and peered through. I wish I hadn't.

The flames were orange, the smoke black, but I could still see the candles, somehow unaffected by the fire, and the skull, which had turned one hundred and eighty degrees, turned toward me. In my periphery, I sensed other things too, things not Brad or Lexi.

The smoke spilled from the shack and into my lungs, like the fire was in me now, and I didn't remember fainting until I woke.

The first thing I noticed were the marks on my arms.
Red streaks of raised flesh that itched horribly. I scratched at them but it only worsened the sensation of things crawling beneath the surface. Blood beaded and something greenish like pus poured from the wound. Maybe I'd fallen on poison sumac or the cats had thought I was down for good. The marks were no doubt infected. I needed a doctor and some water. My tongue was facing a draught.

When I stood, when the dizzy spell passed, I saw the shack was just cinder now, some of it still burning, like embers in a campfire. In the center of the ruin, the candles still wept their flames but the skull was gone. So was the rest of the group. I found no sign of their bodies and when I trekked back to the site, I learned all of our gear had been taken, cameras included. Our movie was missing. This troubled me above all else, above even the loss of my friends. My found footage would never be found. There would be no cheap plastic DVD cases, no name above the title. Maybe my sister was right. Maybe I wasn't just a failure to launch but a failure in all things. I had no desire to search the perimeter for the group. I was happy to find an exit and hope for the best, hope they'd managed to escape the burning shack and Cat Town, that what I'd seen through the gap was just a mirage brought on by bad weed.

The cats rustled as I scratched my new rashes. The lesions has spread from wrist to elbow and darkened from red to brown. My scalp tingled too. I probed my hairline and felt two new welts.

Horns.

When I screamed, throat raw and thirsty, I sensed them all around me. They stepped from the shadows for the first time and I met the inhabitants of Cat Town.

There were not cats.

Something Pagan
Lucas Mangum

The limousine crossed Hewitt onto West Ninth. All the vibrant bar fronts and boutique shops lining East Ninth gave way to dark houses, lit only by silver streetlamps. The lights themselves were designed to look old-fashioned, ovals of luminescence on top of posts made of corrugated black metal. In the darkness between the haloes, everything was a shade of midnight blue.

To Pola, it looked like something out of a Gothic fantasy, the sort of black-and-white mood piece made famous by Val Lewton in the 1940s, colorized slightly and deliberately to keep the vibe.

Pola had seen *Cat People* at least two dozen times, had the menacing green claw of *The Leopard Man* tattooed on her left butt cheek, and knife-wielding Boris Karloff from *Isle of the Dead* featured prominently in a sleeve of Karloff characters inked up her right arm.

This was her first time out to West Ninth, though she'd glimpsed it across Hewitt on her first few weekends in the city. Back then—as she now thought of it, though

114

only three weeks had passed—partying had been her sole priority.

And party, she had. Perhaps a little too hard. It didn't take long at all for the money to dry up. Now her share of the rent was due, and she wasn't about to ask for a loan. She had too much pride for that. Plus, she had plenty of assets she could leverage to come up with the money quick.

Back then, West Ninth held a strange allure, the sort she often felt when sighting dark streets that she never intended to visit, but already her narrative was reshaping itself, telling her she'd suspected she would eventually end up here from the moment she saw it from the opposite side of Hewitt. That she had felt it calling to her but simply hadn't known it at the time. That its dense atmosphere was both exactly what she expected and something so much more. The former truth, that she had no expectations at all on those initial nights, soon became as dark as the spaces between the homes on West Ninth, spaces untouched by the streetlamp haloes or even the light of the moon.

The limousine pulled into a cobblestone driveway tucked away from the rest of the homes. The path wound up the side of a hill, between dense walls of oaks and pines. More of those old-fashioned lampposts were placed at intervals, hanging like ghostly eggs in the nighttime woods.

Pola had told no one where she was going tonight. That flew in the face of common wisdom when it came to women braving the night alone. Hundreds of think pieces and perhaps millions of social posts had been written about how women should let their friends and family know where they are at all times because *men* were dangerous. Worse still, they were *everywhere* and *only after one thing*.

This wasn't entirely off the mark either; the inherent truth underlying this discourse was something Pola knew all too well. Unfortunately, that advice only applied to women who had friends and family to tell. Her roommates barely tolerated her.

Pola wasn't afraid, though. At barely twenty-two, life had already managed to put her through the wringer. Whatever tonight had in store for her, she could handle it. And by the time it was over, she'd be ten-thousand dollars richer.

Or she'd be dead.

The car stopped between a massive marble fountain and an even more massive house. A statue of a woman stood at the fountain's center with her arms outstretched as if preparing to embrace someone. Pola couldn't make out much else from the back of the limo, so she turned toward the house. It was a Victorian, complete with huge windows and cupolas. The front door was Van Gogh yellow and lit in such a way as to accentuate the vivid cow piss color.

The driver cut the engine and the sudden absence gave her an empty feeling she didn't expect. The back of the limousine became a liminal space filled with weighted silence. The moment could've been less than five seconds or several minutes. The unlatching click followed by a gentle groan as the driver opened the door for her broke her daze.

Once outside, she got a better look at the fountain. The woman depicted as a statue was nude but for a wreath of flowers around her head. Her hair flowed over her shoulders, partly down her back and partly over the tops of her breasts. Water poured from each nipple and from her mouth and eyes. Pola stared and tried to make her mouth form words.

"That's Fernalina," the driver said in a tone that was either sad or simply the way he spoke. It was the first thing he'd said to her since picking her up, so she didn't know what to make of it. "Do you know of her?" he asked.

Pola shook her head dumbly.

His lips pressed together. The expression wasn't quite a smile. There was a sense he was adjusting himself somewhere behind his face, of struggling to keep everything together. Perhaps it wasn't discomfort at all, but a means of holding back a laugh, though Pola couldn't imagine what might be so funny.

"Come," he said, gesturing toward the front of the house.

Pola gave the statue's weeping eyes one last look before turning toward the yellow door. She followed the driver to it, assuming he would come in with her, but on the front stoop, he turned and held out a small white envelope.

"This is the key."

"Oh…"

"You'll be letting yourself in. I've other things to attend to, as you must imagine."

"Okay…"

He placed the envelope in her hand.

"It was a pleasure to meet you, Ms. Pola. We'll meet again, I'm sure."

"Um…"

"Charmed," he said and gave her a quick bow.

She watched him walk from the house back to the limo. He didn't look her way again, not even to wave. Once he shut himself inside, she faced the house. She took out the key and examined it. It was brass and otherwise nondescript.

This is a mistake. Right?

Yes, this is too weird. I need to just leave this key on the stoop, walk away, and call someone for a ride.

And beg someone to front me the money for this month?

Yeah, fuck that.

She put the key in the door and turned it.

The inside cut a stark contrast to the exterior. Light from gaudy chandeliers brought everything into hyperfocus—everything from the brown shag carpet with fibers so long they nearly hid her booted feet to the two red velvet armchairs which looked like they'd been constructed for someone seven feet tall. A bookcase stood against the wall to her left. It was full of leatherbound volumes, all of them thick. She recognized none of the titles; some weren't even in English.

At the center of the room stood a grand piano, constructed from wood so polished she could see her reflection in it from several paces back. On the wall opposite the bookcase hung an acrylic painting, its subject bore a striking resemblance to the woman in the fountain.

The silence of the chamber had physical weight, making the air feel dense. It was oddly chilly in the room, though it was warm outside and she neither heard nor felt any of the tell-tale signs of air conditioning. It was as if the cold from the previous winter had been contained here.

Or perhaps this house was the source of the cold.

That was an odd thought. Where could she have come up with that? A house that can control the weather? That was *beyond* odd, it was silly. The placid expression on Fernalina's face suggested otherwise.

Pola set the key on an entry table and stepped further into the house. Her footsteps made whispers on the thick carpet. She called out, "Hello?" No one answered. She took two more steps, passing the piano. The fallboard was lifted, revealing all eighty-eight keys. The white ones reminded her of teeth.

She continued forward, her call still unanswered. When she reached the arched passage leading out of the foyer, a shape stepped out to intercept her.

She jumped back with a gasp, breath and heartbeat quickening in less than half a blink. The shape had emerged so suddenly, it could have only meant to ambush her. And you didn't ambush someone unless you meant them harm.

Coming here was a terrible idea.

What was I thinking?

No amount of money is worth my life.

She staggered back, the shape before her not yet calibrated in her panicked vision. Her left ankle rolled, but she kept her feet. She meant to spin on her heel and make for the door, but a hand reached out and snatched her by the upper arm, right where knife-wielding Boris met the flat top of Frankenstein's monster. She tried to jerk free, but the grip was too strong.

"Hey!" The yelp of protest died on her tongue. "Oh…"

The hand released her. The disparate fragments came together as Pola's alarm receded. They formed a woman, a lithe brunette with a healthy glow to her skin and eyes like sunflowers. She wore a shimmering green dress.

As Pola studied her, a lilting delicate tune began to play on the piano. No one was sitting on the bench, yet the keys moved as if someone were playing them. Pola's mouth fell open in tired shock.

"I didn't mean to startle you," the woman said. Pola faced her again. Her crimson lips drew Pola's attention. They were stoplight red, and Pola didn't think they were painted on. They looked naturally vibrant, but that couldn't be right.

"I'm Lisa," the woman said and held out a hand in greeting.

Pola took it and shook. Her gaze wandered to the piano. The keys depressed and lifted like invisible fingers danced along them. The melody teetered between upbeat and melancholy. It made Pola think of toys left out in the rain.

"How are you doing that?"

Those intense lips smirked. "Just a parlor trick. Do you like the song?"

"I'm not sure."

"I think we'll get along well, Pola," Lisa said with a humorless laugh.

"Are you the one who … hired me?"

"I am. I take it you were expecting a man?"

Pola looked down and to the side. "Maybe."

"I hope that's not a problem."

"No, I just…" She fumbled for the right thing to say. Her gaze fell to where the woman had grabbed her. The skin was pink under the two Karloff characters. "I hope the tattoos are okay."

The woman's lips spread further, becoming a full smile. It should've been disarming, but it only unsettled Pola further. The teeth were as white as those piano keys and way too straight.

She took Pola by the wrist and looked up her arm at all the Karloff faces, at the black star above each collar bone, and the thorny vines etched up her left forearm.

"Every mark tells a story, especially the ones we give to ourselves. These suit you." She let go of Pola's wrist and gestured toward the archway. "Come."

As big as the first room was, there was still a lot of the house left to see. Going through the arched threshold brought them into a hallway lit with uniform sconces designed to look like torches. They hung from the mouths of sculpted screaming faces that protruded from the wall.

As soon as Pola followed Lisa through, the music stopped. It was quiet enough for her to hear her pulse tapping between her ears.

Looking down each way gave Pola the feeling she got in hotel room hallways, a sense of endless chambers and no exit. Such passages always gave her the creeps. She thought it was something more primal than watching *The Shining* too many times; it was something older and innate.

This hallway didn't have too many doors. It didn't have a nearly flat carpet displaying a variety of abstract shapes. Instead, it had five doors total, two on one side and three on the other. The shag carpet of the previous room had been replaced by strong-looking hardwood that was dark in color, nearly black. Pola realized all the screaming faces on the wall belonged to women.

Across the hall was another archway, this one leading to a staircase that went both up and down. A basement. How many houses in this area had those? It made her think there was a purpose for it in this particular house.

"Which way?" Pola asked when she could no longer stand the silence.

Lisa led her to the room with the staircase. Dread coiled in Pola's guts, threatening panic. If Lisa tried to take her to the basement, she'd run right out of here, no question.

A series of frightful scenarios crossed her mind. She imagined Lisa shoving her down the stairs to her death. She imagined an unfinished basement with dead naked women strapped to tables—women who, in life, had been like her, made reckless by a desperate situation. She imagined chained up beasts that were once human but now only knew feral hunger.

Thankfully, Lisa walked past the stairs, between two more doorways—one leading to a kitchen/dining room, the other to another sitting room—and toward a glass door. She slid the door open and ushered Pola onto a concrete patio.

The backyard was just as impressive as the rest of the house. It had a sprawling well-kept lawn that stretched to a wall of hedges standing twelve feet tall. Perfect for privacy. Thick trees stood on either end of the yard. There was a pool, a hot tub, a cabana, and a fancy-looking grill. All of it was lit low, giving the space a hazy, dreamlike feel.

Several other girls sat on the patio furniture. At least one looked like she might be underage. There were four in total.

A brunette sat on the chaise, her open posture was meant to exude confidence, but she had something fragile about her—a wariness and a weariness that Pola could only glimpse by looking directly into her eyes. Detecting Pola's gaze, the brunette quickly looked away.

There were two blondes who looked like twins, fresh-faced and petite, both wearing pink skirts and tops striped pink and white. They had the look of college co-eds, rocking side ponytails pointed the opposite way to distinguish one from the other. Pola wondered if it was an act or just how the apparent sisters always dressed.

The youngest looking had jet-black hair. It looked natural, unlike Pola's which was auburn whenever she let it grow out past the roots. Despite being the apparent youngest, she oozed a self-assuredness that was neither put on, like that of the brunette, or naïve like that of the twins. She gave off the impression that she didn't yet trust Pola, as if there was some as-yet-unrevealed litmus test to pass before the girl fully welcomed her into … whatever this was.

"Is this an audition or something?" Pola asked.

The two blondes exchanged a glance. When they faced forward again, they were bright-eyed and smirking like they found her question funny. The brunette still hadn't looked at her again. The black-haired girl hadn't stopped looking at her. Lisa placed a gentle hand on Pola's shoulder.

"No audition," she said. "You're here because I want you here."

Pola gave each of the other girls another once over. She slipped out of Lisa's hold, trying not to make a show of it but doing just that.

"Look, I don't want to do anything…" she paused and glanced at the black-haired girl who now scowled at her. "…illegal."

"You think you're here for an orgy?" the black-haired girl said with a dry laugh.

The two blondes tittered. The brunette shifted, faced Pola for a blink, then looked away again.

"You're not here for anything sexual," Lisa said.

"But…" Pola started but Lisa held up a silencing hand.

"I'm well aware what was communicated, but I'm saying now that you're here for something much more rewarding."

Pola tried to read the enigmatic host's eyes. "I'm not getting paid, am I?"

"Oh, you'll be paid. In something far more valuable than money."

"Yeah…" Pola scanned the other girls for some sign that this might be a joke. They all wore neutral expressions, even the brunette. Pola came back to Lisa. "That's all well and good, but rent's due and I don't think my landlord takes payment in 'enlightenment' or whatever it is your selling."

Lisa only smiled and gestured back the way they'd come. "You are, of course, under no obligation to stay."

"Right." Pola hesitated. She wanted to tell this smug bitch that she should pay her at least something for coming all the way out here, but at this point, she just wanted to be done with the whole ordeal. She wanted a bed and a shot of something strong to help put her out. She'd talk to her roommates about the rent in the morning. They'd figure something out. "Well, thanks for nothing."

She turned but couldn't take a single step toward the door. Someone was coming through.

The figure was pushing what looked like a gurney. And it wasn't empty. She stared as the gurney clattered over the threshold and onto the patio. The man pushing it was the same individual who'd driven her to this strange house.

Another man was strapped to the gurney with a ball gag in his mouth. She recognized him immediately.

Pola didn't one day simply decide to fall through the cracks. For those cracks to even form required a buildup of pressure such that a surface could no longer keep its shape. It took time for a crack to open wide enough for someone to slip through at all. Once that happened, one still needed to come to the edge, and either be pushed or take a willing leap.

The fracture into which Pola eventually plunged began its formation when she was still a child—though sometimes in the grip of an all-too-frequent sleepless night, she convinced herself it started even earlier than that, as if the product of a family curse or some cruel form of predestination. But her ultimate plunge over the edge came directly as a result of the man who now lay prone before her. He recognized her, too, and his eyes pulled wide with naked terror.

"I can see you two have met," Lisa said. Her tone indicated that she already knew this.

"What is this?" Pola said, feeling like she'd been wondering the same thing all fucking night.

"This is Joel Hutchinson," the black-haired girl said. "But you knew that. How could you not know the name of the asshole who ruined your life? Though, let's face it: you were well on your way to ruin before he came around."

"Where was it you knew him from?" one of the blondes asked.

"They were both exhibitors at a regional horror convention," the other one said.

"Back home," the black-haired girl sneered.

"Oh, right," said the first blonde. "He made jewelry, and she sold used VHS tapes of forgotten horror movies. Is that about right?"

"How do you all know so much about me?" Pola asked.

The black-haired girl rolled her eyes. "Please."

"Be nice, Rena," Lisa said. "We don't want to chase her away."

"Well, then you are failing miserably," Pola blurted, well-past giving a shit whether or not she got paid and reasonably sure she wouldn't see a dime no matter what she said or did. "I don't know what kind of sick shit—"

"Revenge," Lisa said. "We're into revenge, specifically helping people like you find closure through taking vengeance for wrongs visited upon them. Look at him." Lisa put one arm around Pola's shoulders and gestured toward Joel with the other. "Do you mean to tell me seeing him tied down like that doesn't give you *ideas?*"

Joel squirmed as much as he could in his leather restraints and screamed against the ball gag.

"Scream all you want," Rena said. "No one's going to hear you."

The brunette hadn't spoken yet, but Pola caught her staring. She nodded toward the bound man, then looked away. Pola faced Joel again, and he whimpered. He whimpered just like she had, that time he'd followed her out to her car after a long weekend of exhibiting, pressed her against the driver's side door, and kissed her without asking. Then, he'd done a lot worse than that—and she'd done a lot more than whimper. But in the dark parking lot of a mall that wasn't quite dead but certainly on life support, no one had heard her.

When he finished, she slumped down to the pavement. He pulled his jeans back on and told her if she said a word about it to anyone he'd kill her.

As if she could tell anyone. He was a big deal at the popup market where they met—the nephew of the dude who put it all together. She was just some weird girl who barely talked to anybody. Even in the era of #MeToo, both those things would work against her as far as anyone in that circle taking her story seriously went.

The noises of discomfort Joel made brought memories of her own discomfort flooding back. But they also stirred something else within her.

"You want to see him suffer, don't you?" Lisa asked. "You want to see him die for what he did."

She heard his voice in her head now, as clear as she'd heard it that night in the parking lot with gravel digging into her knees and palms, as her entire body trembled with shame, fear, and primal rage: *If you tell anyone about this, I'll fucking kill you.*

The other women were chanting something in unison, their tones hushed. Joel struggled against his restraints as the driver loomed over him, staring into his terror-stricken face.

"You have the chance now to make him pay," Lisa said. "And to stop him from doing the same thing to someone else."

A wave of intoxication overtook Pola. It was sudden and intense, the way she sometimes got if she smoked weed after she'd already been drinking, but with a stark sense of lucidity.

Her vision swam and her insides churned. She couldn't imagine what could've possibly brought this sensation on. She'd been careful not to drink or take anything before heading out for the night. The notion occurred to her that the entire trip, from the drive into the dark part of Ninth to the eerie piano music in the parlor to the chanting of the other women, had brought on her current state. It was as if it had all served as a meticulously choreographed spell, designed to make her susceptible to the whims of Lisa and the others, and to the whims of her dark side, the shadow self that dwelled in her and demanded retribution, demanded blood.

She zeroed in on his throbbing jugular. Inside, pulsated the life force, the life force of an unrepentant sinner.

Lisa put her mouth up to Pola's ear. "Don't you want him to pay for what he's done?"

"Yes," Pola breathed.

Of course, she did. Fantasies of killing Joel Hutchinson in his sleep or luring him in with the promise of "wanting it again" only to stick a knitting needle into his urethra raced through her mind on a semiregular basis. Now that she had the chance to bring those revenge fantasies to life, she could only stand still while the man who raped her lay completely vulnerable, presented for her on a silver platter by Lisa and these other women.

"Have all of you done this?" she asked.

The brunette locked eyes with Pola. "All of us."

Pola focused again on that throbbing vein in his neck. She licked her lips, knowing what Lisa and the others wanted her to do. There were no weapons anywhere nearby. She had only her hands and her mouth.

"You're cannibals," she said, without the revulsion she might have said it with on any other night.

"We only eat the ones who harm us," Lisa said. "But you must take the first bite."

The twins giggled while Joel renewed his muffled screams.

Pola felt like she was in a dream, as if she'd been in a dream all night. This sense that now consumed her made what the others expected of her seem less daunting and less repugnant. She was somewhere that didn't have the same laws and consequences as the real world. This place operated under its own principles and fostered an abandonment of feeling bound to any other rules, including the apparent laws of nature.

"Eat your trauma and become ascended," Lisa said.

Pola's mouth watered, like a smoked brisket lay before her and not a living human being begging for mercy.

"He's not human," Rena said. "He gave that shit up when he raped you."

Pola took a step forward. Joel squirmed against his restraints. The gag kept his cries from reaching beyond the yard. With every step, Pola felt each internal scar fade, her inner workings restored to their pre-trauma stage. But to keep them restored, she had to complete the ritual.

At the side of the gurney, she bent toward Joel's neck. She kept her eyes open, not out of fear that she'd bite somewhere less delectable, but because she wanted to be fully present for this cathartic feast.

When her teeth closed around his skin, he sighed. When they penetrated the flesh, he squealed. She gnawed on the vein, shaking her head side-to-side like a shark with a seal. The blood sprayed her face and his, warm and sticky and oh so red. That was something missing from all those old movies she liked: blood, particularly its lurid color. But this was no film and no dream. This was the beginning of a new life. The beginning of liberation from abuse, trauma, and the cracks that once so characterized her existence.

She ripped a rag of flesh and gristle free and stood up straight, blood dribbling down her chin and pattering the front of her shirt. She swallowed the morsel of vengeance and went back to the convulsing body below for another taste. As she did, the other women joined her.

In her mind's eye, she saw Fernalina in the fountain, the statue's marble contours softening to flesh as the goddess returned to life.

Eaten Alive
J.F. Gonzalez

Averaging in size as large as a dinner plate, the South American Goliath Bird-Eating Spider is the largest spider in the world.

Cindy Jacobs had seventeen specimens in her collection.

They were among one hundred arachnids she kept in various cages in the spare bedroom of the large Tudor-style home she shared with her husband Scott.

Spiders had always been her obsession. Her collection started with a single red-knee tarantula. Thanks to breeding and careful selection from various rare animal dealers, she was able to amass quite a menagerie.

Feeding them was always a problem, though.

The smaller spiders were easy. All she did was pour a bag of crickets into various cages and let nature take its course. For the larger tarantulas, small vertebrates were a necessity and her neighborhood pet store kept a steady supply of pinkie and fuzzy mice on hand.

Feeding the Goliath's was like feeding a small python. She had to kill the mice and small rats she bought for them to avoid damage to her pets.

She didn't mind though. It was all part of the research she was doing.

She stood in the basement of the house watching the Goliaths as they fed. She had taken them downstairs individually in shoeboxes for this experiment, which she'd been working on the past few months. She wanted to prove her own theory that they'd feed on anything.

Accordingly to current scientific data, Goliath's fed on insects and small vertebrates such as frogs, salamanders, lizards, snakes, rodents and birds. This was their natural diet in their native habitat, the jungles of South America. In captivity hobbyists generally offered them small mice. By instinct, the spider sinks its fangs into its victim, injecting it with venom that would render them paralyzed and would immediately begin digestion of the flesh. The spider then sucked all the fluids out of its meal, leaving an empty shell of skin.

The venom of a Goliath Bird-Eating Spider is no more toxic than that of a red-knee tarantula. What made their bite so painful and potentially dangerous was the length of their fangs. At one inch in length, they could inject their venom deep into your muscles, causing severe pain, partial temporary paralysis, and in severe cases partial necrosis of tissue.

Scott had become verbally and physically abusive with her the morning he found that her research with the Goliath's had cost the life of their house cat, Betty. Cindy had been excited when, after starving her two female Goliath's for over two months, they'd lunged at the cat after Cindy lowered her carefully into the bathtub with a set of tongs. She'd released one of the tarantulas into the bathtub moments before and waited till that first one was occupied with sinking its fangs into Betty before releasing the second one, which made a quick lunge for the cat's hindquarters at the first scent of prey. Cindy had hated the cat anyway. Breaking its neck had been relatively easy.

That phase of her experiment proved to be a milestone. Only Scott hadn't been so happy. She'd born the scars from his beating for over a month.

It had taken all her effort and vigilance to keep him out of the room she kept her spiders in. She'd had a locksmith install a special lock on the door months ago. Day jobs kept them away from each other during daylight hours. His philandering and drinking kept him from the house at night, leaving her to continue her research and plan the current phase of her experiment.

It had been hard to starve all seventeen of her Goliaths, but it was the only method she knew of to create a sense of ravenousness in them. All of the experts in arachnids unanimously agreed that spiders – especially tarantulas – would not eat prey that was larger than themselves, even if they were starving. Cindy had proven that theory wrong with Betty.

She was proving it now with Scott, who lay paralyzed on the basement floor. She'd taken him down with one well-placed Tai-Kwon Do kick that snapped his neck, severing his spinal cord, and she'd waited till he regained consciousness before she started bringing the Goliath's down one by one.

The pain and horror in his eyes was evident as the first one crawled tentatively on his stomach and then stabbed its fangs into his flesh.

The rest had followed suit as she released them.

Now as she stood watching as babies feed she wondered how many feedings it would take for Scott to be completely desiccated.

A Little Something
Scott Cole

"Sounds like you had a pretty good day," Ellen said.

She slid one last bite of brisket between her lips and chewed it heartily, enjoying it just as much as she had the first mouthful. Over the years, many of her friends had complained that they didn't like their own cooking, or that they got desensitized to the aromas during the process, but she always enjoyed whatever she made.

Her husband, John, was savoring the meal too. She flashed him a warm smile across the table. She adored him.

"Mmm. Yeah, it *was* a good one. Insanely busy, but very productive," John said, with the final bite from his own plate tucked into one cheek. "I think we may have locked down a new account." He returned his wife's smile, swallowed, then stood up abruptly and began clearing the table. John's sudden movement startled Ellen, but the feeling was momentary. She reached for her wine glass and finished what remained of her Cabernet.

The plates and silverware rattled as John piled everything up—though it was clear he was attempting to handle the task as delicately as possible—and the stack continued to clatter as he moved into the kitchen to set it all down inside the sink. "I'll wash these later, okay?"

"Oh, I can do them," Ellen responded. "I don't mind. You had a long day. You're probably pretty wiped out."

"No, no. You put that beautiful meal together," John said. "The least I can do is handle the dishes."

Much of their home was an open floor plan, so he remained in Ellen's sight the whole time. When she glanced at him across the room now, she was filled with a rush of tenderness. She loved him so much. But more importantly, he was enough. He was *more* than enough. He was everything to her. Their life together hadn't been perfect, nor had it necessarily gone the way they had planned from the beginning, but it didn't matter, as long as they had each other.

John turned back around from the sink and stepped forward to the border between the kitchen and dining areas. When he paused, Ellen detected the slightest hint of a grin.

"I just meant I have something for you," John said. "And I can't wait any longer."

Ellen loved that devilish, mischievous look he sometimes got, and the twinkle in his eye that accompanied it. She shifted sideways in her chair, squaring her body toward him, propping one arm over the wooden back and cocking her head slightly.

"Oh?" she said in a playful tone. She suddenly felt the warmth of the wine in her cheeks. "What have you done?"

John's smile filled out as he walked back across the dining area and into what they often referred to as the living room, even though the entire first floor was one large open space, mainly divided by the positioning of furniture. He approached the wing chair in the corner, where he had left his shoulder bag.

"I picked up a little something today," he said. "After work." Ellen spun to the other side of her chair and watched as John gripped the top of the black faux-leather bag and pulled the zipper across. The bag yawned open. John spread the two sides wider.

"Seriously, honey. What have you done?" Ellen's tone remained lighthearted. It's not that she didn't want the surprise. Her heart swelled at the idea that her husband— this wonderful, thoughtful, caring man—had taken time out of his busy day to do something for her.

"Well, I decided to take a little detour on my way home," John said. He looked back to his wife as he extracted a black rectangular container from the shoulder bag.

Ellen screwed her face and squinted at her husband as one side of her mouth began to curl up the side of her face. She recognized the container immediately as the soft, insulated box he often used to transport his lunches to work.

John returned to the dining area and placed it down gently on the table in front of her.

"And what is this?" Ellen said, puzzled. "Dessert?"

"Go ahead, open it," John replied, nodding toward the box.

Ellen paused, then undid the zipper that ran around three sides of the puffy container's top panel. Raising the flap and peeking over the edge, she found a gray plastic shopping bag inside, its handles tied shut. A plastic icepack sat beside it, still surprisingly cold.

She stopped for another moment, then untied the bag without removing it, only to find another inside, this one white, its handles also twisted together in a knot.

"This is a joke, right?" she said, shooting John a look that said *We Are Not Amused*. He stood to the left of her, one hand on the edge of the table, the other on the back of her chair. "How many of these am I going to have to go through?"

"Not a joke," he said. "And you're almost there. Last one."

Ellen rolled her eyes and untied the knot. She did not see another plastic bag inside.

She glanced up at her husband again, who remained perched over her shoulder. He nodded once again toward the container.

Ellen had to lean forward slightly in order to see what was inside. When she did, she gasped, and John's smiled widened at her reaction.

"Is this—? *Oh my god, John!*" Ellen's cheeks flushed immediately. She covered her mouth with one hand and gripped her husband's wrist with the other. "Where did you—?"

"I cut through the park on my way home."

"Oh my god. Oh my *god.* Is this...*is this a left?*"

John dipped his head in affirmation. His eyes sparkled. "It is."

Ellen took a huge breath in. "Oh, it's *wonderful!*"

"You sure? You like it?"

"Are you kidding? Of course! It's beautiful!" Ellen jumped up from her chair and gave John a hug. "I love you, honey. It's absolutely perfect."

"I love you too," John said. He kissed her forehead first, then pressed his lips against hers. They stood in silence for a moment, embracing tightly, stopping time, just as they had after exchanging their wedding vows nine years earlier.

"Shall we get started then?" John whispered into Ellen's ear. "Or do you want to wait 'til tomorrow?"

Ellen took a breath and wiped a tear from the corner of one eye. Then she placed both of her palms on her husband's chest and looked him firmly in the eyes, smiling as wide as ever.

"No, let's do it tonight," she said.

"I was hoping you'd say that."

They squeezed each other again, then broke their embrace. Ellen began to clear more space on the table, while John stepped into the garage. He returned a few moments later with four large Ziploc bags and a separate, somewhat larger plastic-wrapped bundle, all of which were slightly clouded.

"I pulled these out of the deep freeze when I got home," he said. "Everything looks like it's mostly defrosted already." He set each of the bags down gently, then disappeared into the garage again.

Ellen chuckled and shook her head, then reached into the shopping bags inside the lunch box to remove the gift her husband had brought home. It was a beautiful thing—a left arm, small but chubby, its fingers curled loosely into a tiny fist—a baby's left arm, cool to the touch, but still soft and pink, except at the shoulder, where it was red and ragged, except for some lavender bruising and an exposed knob of white bone. There was some crimson slop in the bottom of the bag, but it wasn't as messy as she would have expected.

She tried to imagine what John had done to obtain such a nice-looking limb. From the looks of things, he'd had a minute or two to make a relatively clean cut, all things considered. So that was good—both for them and the donor. The child he had encountered would probably heal up just fine. She knew the park he had referred to, and it wasn't far from a hospital. Her husband was always such a thoughtful man, always keeping logistics and efficiency in mind.

"Honey?" John called from the garage. "I've got the gloves, but I don't see the…"

Ellen was lost in her thoughts, though. She removed the contents of the four freezer bags—a pair of legs, a head, and a right arm the same size as the left—then she unrolled the torso from the larger sheet of plastic. All baby parts. All roughly proportionate.

She thought back. It was just a few years ago, though it seemed it could've been a decade or more.

The right leg had been the first piece. John had taken it from that little boy at the beach, where they had been vacationing. The child had approached them—not the other way around—crawling across the sand, obviously confused and upset, though unable to verbalize it beyond a few chirps and moans. John had picked the boy up into his arms and gone in search of a panicked parent, but even after an hour of looking, there was no one to be found.

That's when the process had begun. John had considered taking the boy home whole, he later told Ellen, but ultimately decided against it, knowing there would never be any easy way to explain to their friends and neighbors why this small child—a total stranger—was suddenly living with them.

They had never wanted to adopt anyway. They wanted their own child.

John had taken the boy over behind the dunes, where he pressed the child's face into the sand and twisted his leg sharply, before tugging it up and outward, snapping the joint as if he was separating a drumstick from a Thanksgiving turkey. The skin had bruised instantly and started to split, but it wasn't quite enough. John used the sharp edge of a seashell like a scalpel, slicing into the soft young skin, then sawing back and forth through the meat and connective tissue beneath, making the separation of the limb easier. It was quick, and much simpler than John would have expected. There wasn't even that much blood, really—or at least the sand absorbed most of it in a matter of seconds. He wrapped the child's leg in the towel he'd been carrying over his shoulder. Then he kicked sand onto the kid's gored shoulder and left him there. And that was that.

Back at the hotel, they placed the leg in the freezer, and then packed it with ice from the machine down the hall for the trip home. And then into the deep freeze it went.

They had come upon the other parts in a variety of ways in the few years since.

The right arm had originally belonged to a baby girl left alone in her mother's car, in a parking lot outside a busy shopping center. The window had been left cracked—thank goodness for that—and it was open just wide enough for

Ellen to reach in with her own slender arm and unlock the door. The serrated blade on the multitool in her pocket had made the job quick and easy.

The left leg came from a baby who had seemingly been abandoned on the changing station of a dingy rest stop bathroom. Ellen had always imagined those sorts of places to be active, jammed with busy travelers, but for some reason there weren't many people on that particular highway that day.

The body—the torso—had come from a small child running rampant around a public pool Ellen and John had visited one brutal summer. Not unlike the little boy at the beach a couple years before, this child appeared to be unsupervised, and was therefore easy for them to abscond with.

As for the head, John had never told Ellen exactly how he had come upon that. She couldn't get over how adorable the face was, with its little dimples and chubby cheeks.

"Oh, never mind," John called again from the garage. "I found them."

He returned to the kitchen, where he found his wife crying silently.

"Ellen? Babe, what's wrong?" he asked, concerned, dropping the things in his arms and racing to her side. The spool of surgical thread hit the hardwood and rolled slowly to the baseboard as he enrobed her in his arms and held her tight. Ellen sobbed into his shoulder and squeezed him back even stronger than before.

"I'm just so *happy*," she said with a sniffle. "You know I've wanted to be a mother for so long. I just—I never thought it was going to happen."

John rocked her softly back and forth for a moment, then lurched back to meet her eyes with his own.

"I know," he said, wiping tears from his wife's cheeks. "And you're going to be fantastic."

Ellen sobbed again and chuckled through her tears. She took a deep breath and dabbed the wetness from her face with a napkin. Then she took another, deeper breath and cleared her throat, as if to punctuate the moment like a new beginning. A clean slate.

"You ready?" John whispered a moment later, letting go of their embrace. She nodded and smiled wide, her eyes glistening.

John picked the supplies up from the floor. He tugged a pair of rubber gloves from a cardboard box and handed them over to his wife, then pulled two more out for himself and snapped them onto his own hands. Then he began threading a needle.

"Okay then," he said, excited that the moment was finally here. "Let's make a baby."

Do You Have Splatterpunk?
Carver Pike

"Do you have splatterpunk?"

It should have been such a simple question.

I was plunged into the horror that night. Thrown right in like a kid who can't swim tossed into a lake by a deadbeat dad who wants to prove his machismo by making the boy kick to the surface with death nipping at his heels.

Only my dad isn't a deadbeat. He's somebody important. Turns out, he's what got me into this mess. Let me back up a bit.

Chicago has always been an electrified city. That's how I've always described it. From the moment I stepped foot on the Magnificent Mile and saw the bright holiday lights, felt the freezing wind whipping off the nearby lake, and heard the honking of horns, I knew life was about to change.

I was alive. Everyone was. Sure, depression followed me there like it did every place else, but this was different. I could rest my hand on a park bench, close my eyes, and feel the pulse of the city. It thump-thumped along as God strummed the pedestrian veins and arteries, turning the entire metropolis into a moving kaleidoscopic concert of semi-controlled chaos.

It was a beautiful thing. Until it wasn't. I'll get to that in a moment.

Life in Chi-Town was… different. My apartment had no parking space, but I'd known better than to bring a car so that was fine.

At twenty-two years old, I was single, and I was ready to try my hand at living in the big city.

Not daring enough to swing it in the Big Apple.

Nah, fuck that shit. That place is too wild.

But I was in a big city, nonetheless.

I'd always been an avid reader. My genre was mostly fantasy. Tolkien, of course, but also George R.R. Martin, Joe Abercrombie, and Brent Weeks. I dabbled in horror from time to time. King by default. Who hadn't read King? I'd even tried Koontz, Straub, and Keene. Some of the new bestsellers had caught my eye like Josh Malerman, Grady Hendrix, and Paul Tremblay. That was about as deep as I dared dive in the horror pool.

I kept my floaties on if you know what I mean.

One other thing about Chicago was there was a coffee shop on nearly every corner. There were the big commercial spots but also much smaller fare, too. My favorite was a place called Books & Beans.

That's where I was the Thursday night it all started.

And it started, my experience with it, with a guy named Holbrook Johns. Now, after the fact, I know that he was a part of an online book group. Some kind of Facebook thing I believe. It was for fans of what they call extreme horror and splatterpunk.

I'd just sat down with an apple fritter and a plain, boring latte. My book for the night was something from Reese Witherspoon's club. For the life of me, I can't remember the title now. It disappeared in all the ruckus.

Ruckus seems like such a trite word to describe it. Tactless really. Forgive me.

This wasn't two people arguing over the last item at a Black Friday sale.

The book was lost in all the bloodshed, and it never seemed important enough to try and find it or even buy another copy.

What I do remember are the other patrons in the café.

Two women sat together talking loudly about their recent trip to a nail salon. It irked me because I didn't care how overpriced they thought it was or how they wished they'd gone to the place on South Loop where they could've also gotten facials for the same price. Their volume was rude.

A man with a receding hairline, wearing one of those vests that looks like a life preserver – probably made by The North Face, talked business on his phone. He was a day trader conducting business at night. He, too, spoke at an unreasonably high decibel.

The café area near the front of the store was always busy with people less likely to be engaged in reading. They were more occupied with being their best, or arguably their worst, social selves. Only one of the nine I counted actually had a book on her.

It was then I decided I was best suited for the rear of the store, the actual bookstore side, which was lined with bookshelves, cozier furniture, and dimmer lighting. I carried my snack and my drink to an armchair with a table beside it and sat. Incredibly, the sound from the front of the store seemed muffled back here.

Seated in an olive-green loveseat against the far wall was a muscular man who minded his own business while he drank an iced coffee and read a bright neon orange book that had something to do with the art of not giving a fuck. He represented the book well as he ignored the other annoying patrons.

Note to self. Buy a copy of that book.

I seemed to completely give a fuck... entirely too much.

142

Even from my new spot in the far back, my eyes darted from left to right, dancing over the many coffee sippers up front as they chewed their scones, dabbed at corners of their mouths with napkins, and talked about city life with friends sitting across the table from them or lovers on the other end of a phone screen.

I hadn't even finished a full page of my book and several people had come and gone.

Have I always been like this? So easily annoyed by others?

I didn't think so. It was like my senses were on high alert.

There had to be at least fifteen people inside Books & Beans when the bell above the door jingled that last time.

When *he,* Holbrook Johns, walked in, drenched from a downpour I hadn't even realized existed. The rear of the store was cut off from the outside world, away from the windows, in a dark cave of sorts.

Nobody else seemed to notice the newcomer, but my eyes were locked on him, and I was thankful he didn't see me. He had to stand over 6'3" and weigh over three hundred pounds. His long, brown overcoat was soaked through and was unbuttoned to reveal a T-shirt that read: *The Scream.* It had a red electric guitar on it and at the bottom the words were mostly covered by the jacket, but it looked like it might be either a movie reference or a book.

It read: By

Beneath that and between the flaps of the jacket were the letters: n Skipp and Craig Spe

Holbrook's wet, stringy hair was pasted to his pale head like roots from a tree that must've been invisible atop his head. Rainwater dripped from those strands, running down his wide cheeks like rivers of sweat. The skin around his eyes was red, like he'd been rubbing at them the way a small child does when they're tired and ready for bed.

His grey sweatpants were soaked through, and it didn't appear that he was wearing any underwear. The outline of his member was on full display. He was well-endowed. I didn't mean to look, but it seemed propped against his thigh as if purposely put on display. Yet a closer look at the man would tell you not much about him was done on purpose. He was about as sloppy and unkempt as a person could get.

On his feet were flipflops. That was the oddest thing of all. He'd gone out into the city streets in what seemed to be a torrential downpour, fully clothed, but in flipflops.

I looked back at the bodybuilder on the loveseat to see if he'd noticed the newcomer. He hadn't. He was still dedicated to his art.

The big man at the store's entrance stepped my way, passing the two women with fresh manicures. One of the ladies looked up at him, sniffed, and scowled. He'd apparently given off a foul odor. She gestured to her friend with a nod of her head toward the door, signaling that they should leave. Her friend laughed and held up a finger. One second. She returned to the text message she was working on.

Loud *thuds* followed by the *squish-squish* of his flipflops reaching the carpeted floor of the bookstore side of the business brought chills to my bones. In order to purchase books, one would have to visit the cashier counter nearest me, which put Holbrook only about ten feet away from where I sat.

Instinct took over for me, and it saved my life, because I left my plate and coffee mug on the small table next to my chair and stepped deeper into one of the aisles of books, so I could create a greater distance between myself and the large, drenched man.

Thinking back, I wish I would have hurried for the door, but that would have meant passing within a couple of feet of him, and to put it frankly, I was scared. I had no real reason to be at this point, but I was. There was an aura about him. The man terrified me.

From where I stood, staring at the spines of Christian books written by Derek Prince and Joyce Meyer, I overheard the man as he spoke to one of the young cashiers. The kid couldn't have been over the age of eighteen. He had a laid-back attitude. Real softspoken.

"Whoa, you got soaked out there," the kid said.

"It's… it's raining," the man replied. His voice had zero emotion.

"Yeah, I'd definitely say it is. Here, take this towel. It's not much but at least you can dry your face with it."

I couldn't see the interaction taking place, but I thought it was pretty thoughtful of him to offer the man something to dry himself with.

"Yes," the man said.

A few seconds later, the kid finally asked, "So, what brings you into Books & Beans? Is there something I can help you find? Or are you just wanting a hot cup of coffee to warm that chill from the rain?"

"Do… do… do you have splatterpunk?" the man asked.

"I'm sorry?" the kid replied.

At this point, I dared to step up on my toes and peer over the shelf. I caught a glimpse of Holbrook Johns at the counter, standing directly in front of the blond young man wearing a tan Books & Beans visor and apron.

It looked like the big guy was huffing and puffing, breathing angrily as he was forced to repeat himself. "I said, do you have splat… splatterpunk?"

"I don't think so, sir," the kid said. He turned to one of his coworkers and asked. "Hey, Raquelle, do you know if we have splatterpunk?"

"We have steampunk," she said.

The big man shook his head violently, obviously displeased with the answer. "I said splatterpunk."

"Yeah," the kid said. "We don't have that. I mean if there's a certain book you're looking for, I can probably order it for you and—"

It happened fast. So fast.

I still can't say where he produced the hatchet. It might have been up his sleeve or maybe in an inside jacket pocket. Perhaps tucked in his waistband.

The boy was offering to help order the book and then—

Thwack.

The hatchet blade hit him in the middle of the forehead.

I froze in place.

Around me, the world kept moving.

Raquelle, the coworker, had turned and was talking to a customer about heating up a cinnamon roll.

Everyone else continued with their asinine conversations.

This boy was bleeding profusely from a gigantic gash in his skull, and nobody even noticed.

"And you won't even believe what that dunce said next," some old lady prattled on.

"Happy birthday to you," a middle-aged gentleman sang to the party on the other side of his video screen.

"I'm not kidding, Paul," a young woman started loud but then lowered her voice as she continued with, *"I need to know how serious you are about me."*

It was unreal. As if my head was tuned in to some foreign radio channel where the words almost didn't make sense, the idiots around me wouldn't shut up. They didn't see what was happening right here in front of me.

In front of them!

Holbrook Johns held onto the hatchet handle like he was roasting a marshmallow over a campfire. He turned his wrist slightly to the left and a little to the right.

My mouth opened to scream, to call out for help, to yell out a warning, to say anything at all, but no words came out. My throat was dry.

"Uh," the kid with the hatchet planted in his skull muttered. It was like his brain hadn't quite locked onto the severity of the situation. "Uh."

"What the fuck, bro?" came the voice of the body builder seated on the loveseat behind me. "Holy shit!"

He charged at the man, and his act of bravery was astonishing. I was still frozen in place. Raquelle, having heard the commotion, was now turning to see what was happening.

Holbrook Johns yanked the hatchet out of the kid's forehead.

Blood flew from his wound and whipped across Raquelle's face, splattering across the still-cold cinnamon roll.

Still, not a single scream from anyone.

"Somebody grab him from behind!" the body builder yelled as he charged head-on at the behemoth standing at the counter.

Nobody moved to help. How could they? Why would they when they didn't understand what was happening?

The body builder had to be more powerful than the overweight psycho, but Holbrook Johns wasn't operating with the regular rules that govern society. Whatever this "splatterpunk" was that he was searching for, he was tapping into its energy, and he seemed to be creating in himself whatever the store was lacking.

"Come on, motherfucker!" the body builder yelled as he launched himself at the calm killer with a raised fist.

Holbrook Johns, with incredibly precise aim, flicked his wrist at exactly the right moment and brought the blade down into the spot between the second and third knuckle of the muscular attacker's fist. The hatchet tore through his hand, splitting it right down the center, ripping it in half.

The body builder fell against the counter, holding his bloody hand that burbled like a scarlet brook.

He only had a second to cry out and witness the carnage that had become his own knuckles before Holbrook brought the hatchet around once more and whacked it into the fleshy part of the neck just above the collar bone. The body builder grunted once. Holbrook pulled the blade free and hit him repeatedly.

Raquelle screamed.

The two ladies with the manicures were the first to run for the door.

Holbrook Johns clip-clopped toward them with his flipflops slapping the floor all the way to the door. They reached the knob fairly quickly but didn't realize he'd locked it upon entering the establishment.

No one did.

The massive monstrosity rushed at them like a bull as he homed in on the woman who'd complained about his scent. He didn't like her. "Ma'am," he called out. "Do you have splatterpunk?"

"Wha... what?" she asked, shaking the door violently.

"It's locked," the other woman said as she turned the lock on the door. She twisted the handle and ran out the door.

The complainer didn't have as much luck. She was about to step through the door when Holbrook Johns ducked down low and brought the hatchet blade up between her legs, splitting her right up the middle. "Splatterpunk!" he yelled.

She screamed and then all I heard were the sounds of his blade biting into wet pieces of flesh.

I'd ducked down behind one of the bookshelves, like a coward, but I'd never been a brave man. Surviving was my goal. Not earning the key to the city. I'd seen what happened to the body builder when he tried to be the hero. He should have paid more attention to the title of his book.

When Holbrook Johns turned from the attack at the door, he stood looking in at the rest of us. From where I was crouched, I couldn't tell how many of *us* remained. The gigantic man blocking the door breathed in and out in heavy breaths. His face and hands were splattered with blood and either sweat or rainwater.

From my left, I heard one of the employees whisper from somewhere behind the counter, "Yes, please… help. He's still in the store. He's going to kill us all. I'll try to stay on the line."

All I could think was – if I could hear her, *he* could hear her.

Next came the *whoosh* of something flying through the air and the *thump* of the collision. The girl on the phone let out an audible, "Ungfff." Then her body hit the floor with a *thud*.

"Please," a man begged in a high-pitched whine. "I have money in my wallet. Over a hundred bucks. I'll give it to you."

"Do you have splatterpunk?" the killer asked calmly.

Surely the cops had to be on their way. Calling them was only going to get me captured. Instead, I opened the web browser on my phone and looked up "examples of splatterpunk."

In the meantime, Holbrook Johns continued to torment his victim in the café.

"Do you have splatterpunk?" Holbrook repeated.

"I'm sorry, but I don't know what that is," the terrified man answered.

Holbrook Johns grumbled.

I raised up high enough to see the victim's balding head as he held his hands out in front of his face and tried to protect himself.

Blood erupted, spraying the man's face and splattering the books behind him, as the hatchet lobbed off nearly every finger from the man's left hand and tore through a couple on the right before getting lodged in one of his knuckles.

He shrieked in agony.

Holbrook Johns shoved the hatchet forward, pressing it through the man's hand and into his chest. The victim cried out and tried to fight back, but he was scrawny compared to the madman shoving him into the bookcase at his back.

The killer yanked back on the hatchet and brought it down repeatedly, hacking away at the man.

A couple of other patrons ran out the door. I was the only one still in the building. It was my only chance to escape.

It was now or never.

Slowly, I made my way toward the door, doing my best not to alert the psycho. It didn't matter. He was finished with his prey, and he turned his attention toward me.

If there hadn't been furniture in my way, I would have raced for the door, but instead, I stopped moving.

Holbrook Johns's eyes zeroed in on me.

His heavy footfalls came my way. Blood dripped from the blade of his hatchet.

"That was awesome!" I said, thinking maybe if I switched up tactics and attempted something none of the others had tried, I might be able to weasel my way out of this. "You are so badass!"

Holbrook growled like a feral animal and continued toward me.

Snapping my fingers to remember what I'd read on my phone, I found the words and shouted, "You're just like Simon in Richard Laymon's *Endless Night*!"

The killer stopped and stared dumbly at me.

"Laymon?" he asked. "You know Laymon?"

"Yeah," I said, quickly scanning the store for the horror section. My eyes landed on the Stephen King books which took up an entire shelf of the two-shelf display. "I came here hoping to find some J.F. Gonzalez, maybe some Edward Lee, or some…" I took a closer look at his shirt which was more visible now. I recognized the names from my quick internet search. "Or some Skipp & Spector."

He eyed me suspiciously, cocking his head to the side like a confused dog. I understood he'd decided to kill everyone in the establishment and was now faced with a conundrum. He'd met "one of his own."

My hands trembled as I pointed a finger at the spines of all the books on one of the horror shelves, trying not to piss myself. From where I stood, I could see the employee who'd tried to call the cops. The object Holbrook had thrown at her was a stone Shakespeare-shaped bookend. It had caved in the right side of her skull.

Holbrook's heavy footsteps alerted me to the fact that he'd followed me into the aisle but remained at the far end. He was still unsure about me.

"It's all King, Poe, Lovecraft..." I managed to glance down at my phone as I peeked at another list of splatterpunk authors. "No Brian Keene, Wrath James White... no Poppy Z. Brite, Christine Morgan, Beauregard, Volpe, Triana..." I had to stop listing names or I'd sound like a jackass.

I only hoped he knew the authors I was mentioning. They could be super famous, or they could be nobodies.

"Do you have splatterpunk?" Holbrook Johns asked.

When I turned to look at him, I saw his nose twitch and his hand tighten around his hatchet handle. His shoulders rose and fell with each of his heavy breaths. It was clear he was looking for an excuse to kill me.

"Yuh... yeah," I said. "I ha... have splatterpunk."

"Where?"

"At home."

"Show me."

My heart dropped. There was no way I was going to take this man to my house. Yet I was terrified to try and outrun him. He might throw that hatchet at my back. For now, I only wanted to live.

"Okay, yeah. I can do that."

He nodded toward the door.

The cops would be arriving any second. I only needed to make it until then. I kept my eyes straight ahead, refusing to peer down at the floor because I knew if I did, I'd see the body builder's mangled corpse.

Even with my gaze focused on the door, it was impossible to ignore the blood. It was sprayed across the windows, splattered on the tabletops, and splashed on every other surface. Dismembered body parts lay strewn about on the floor like meaty souvenirs in a twisted, psychotic art display.

To my left was carnage and to my right was more of the same.

Ahead of me, lying on the floor at the door was the lady who'd been split at her seam. She was still alive somehow and trying to crawl into the café. I wondered if she knew she was going the wrong way. Any hope I had of leaving the door open for her was squashed when she reached Holbrook and grabbed hold of his ankle as if hoping he'd help her.

The big man looked down at her shaking body, blood running down her face and blending with the drool dripping from the corner of her pleading lips.

He lifted one of his meaty feet and brought his flipflop down on the crown of her head, smashing her chin and face into the floor. The rubber sole of the flipflop broke in half and left him with only the top portion clinging to the plastic piece between his toes. Holbrook angrily kicked the broken beach shoe from his foot, leaned over, and buried his hatchet in the woman's right temple. She quit moving.

Holbrook Johns stared down at his feet as if contemplating removing the other flipflop, but he didn't. For some reason, he left it on his foot. This psycho killer had one bare foot, as if he'd just stepped out of the shower, and one looking like he was on his way to the pool. He lifted the foot with the flipflop on it and moved it from side to side, maybe making sure it was still functional.

He lowered his foot, retrieved his weapon, and shoved me. "Go."

Inside, I wanted to scream. On the outside, I forced a smile and said, "Beautiful work."

Outside Books & Beans, the pavement was still wet from the night's downpour. Fresh air hit me and for the first time, I wanted to cry. The blast of cool wind on my face was my first sense of freedom.

Cars honked.

Police sirens wailed, but they were far off. Cops were always responding to crimes in Chicago. It didn't mean they were headed our way.

A blind man shook a cup and seemed to be making his own music with it, playing his Styrofoam maraca only to himself, having no idea of the carnage that had taken place across the street from him.

Don't the blind have heightened senses? Couldn't they hear better than the average sighted person? Or was that only Marvel Comics' Daredevil?

It was clear from the blind man's demeanor that he hadn't heard *shit*.

Didn't the people who'd run from the bookstore call the cops? Surely, they did.

A scream sounded off somewhere in the distance, and Holbrook chuckled from behind me. It was like he knew something I didn't.

His hatchet pressed against my back, prodding me forward, and I once again considered running.

Up ahead and across the street was a fast-food burger joint that was always open and busy at this hour. Tonight, the lights were out. Someone had thrown a big rock through the front window.

A helicopter buzzed by overhead, shining its spotlight down onto the city.

Gunshots erupted from inside a nearby apartment building. I looked toward the five-story structure and saw most of the lights were out. More pops from a pistol and as the firearm barked, one of the windows lit up. Inside that apartment, someone screamed.

Chicago was always a bit hectic. As I mentioned earlier, it was one of the things I enjoyed about it. The haphazardly organized chaos. Frequently visited tourist areas were kept clean and were usually void of crime while the deeper, inner-city neighborhoods played by a different set of rules.

Of course, the cops did their best to keep the peace. They responded to calls and made arrests, but they weren't as actively vigilant as they might be on the Magnificent Mile.

Where I now walked, with a killer pressing the heavy end of his hatchet against the small of my back, was somewhere in-between.

"Splatterpunk?!" I swore I heard someone call out from far away. The word echoed off the walls around us.

Holbrook Johns chuckled behind me.

Coming up on my left was a florist shop. The door was open, and the light inside was on. Dangling from an awning were several potted plants. As we approached, I glanced up at the chains holding them in place. I was short enough to walk under them, but Holbrook would need to duck.

It was the best chance I'd have to escape.

"We could kill the florist," I suggested.

The big killer wheezed behind me.

Only a few feet more.

"What do you think?" I asked, glancing over my shoulder.

He nodded.

We'd reached the first dangling plant. The pot was small. The next would be better, so I kept walking, and as I passed the second plant, I reached up, palmed the pot, and swung it back behind me.

The crash was loud.

Holbrook Johns grunted. "Ungh."

The pot shattered against his head and rained to the ground like pieces of broken glass.

I didn't look behind me to survey the damage. It was time to run. My feet launched me forward and I ran—

But the maniac was fast. Too fast.

The force and searing pain were like a molten hot railroad spike driving through my left shoulder. The hatchet punched me and lodged in bone, spinning me to my left where I ran into the circular glass table of the French diner just beyond the florist.

I hit the surface on my stomach, arms stretched out, and splashed through the glass, taking the table frame with me as I flipped over it and bounced my head off the diner's brick wall.

If I didn't land on the hatchet, pushing it deeper into my shoulder, I might have slipped into unconsciousness. The agony of having my arm nearly severed from my shoulder caused me to shriek. The thuds of Holbrook's heavy footsteps made me get to my knees and crawl across shards of shattered glass, pulling myself along with one good hand.

He must have been toying with me because he could have caught me quickly if he wanted to. Behind me, he nonchalantly tossed a metal chair out of his way, and I heard it clang off the sidewalk. He flung another, swiped a table to the side, kicked a chair, flipped a table. One by one he slowly stalked me.

Ahead, I saw the light of The Soup(er) Bowl, a small take-out restaurant that served only soup mostly in bread bowls. The door was open and the warm glow from inside spilled out onto the sidewalk. If I could only make it through the doorway, maybe I could close and lock the door behind me.

I pulled one foot up under me and shoved upward, standing as tall as I could, and yanked my other foot up. My body wanted to collapse again, so I gripped the wall next to me and staggered on flimsy legs toward The Soup(er) Bowl.

Behind me, the thrashing of my tormentor continued. He was still tossing metallic furniture out of his way.

His bare foot and flipflop beat the wet grass in the small patch of lawn that led toward the door of the soup restaurant.

Holbrook was only ten to fifteen feet behind me when I reached the entrance and fell into the small restaurant. I gripped the knob as I pitched myself through the open doorway and flung the door shut behind me.

With my left arm dangling at my side, I quickly threw the deadbolt with my right hand and watched as Holbrook's large shadow filled the frosted window at the door's center.

There he was, with only a plate of glass separating us.

His hatchet was still buried in my shoulder, but he wouldn't need that to continue his reign of terror. He could easily smash his way through the door. Yet he didn't. His silhouette remained in place.

Behind me, The Soup(er) Bowl was silent.

When I turned around, I expected to see a stunned server staring at me, a strange man covered in blood with a hatchet lodged in his shoulder, but that wasn't the case at all. What I'd thought would be an empty, tidy soup restaurant with a bored cashier was something insanely different.

The walls were splattered with blood.

On the floor, only a few feet in front of me, lay a naked woman who'd been sliced open from her ass crack to the crown of her head. Squatting down next to her was an Asian woman just as naked, her face covered in blood, ladling what appeared to be broccoli and cheddar soup from a bucket into the dead woman's wound. She'd already filled the gap from her ass up to mid-back.

Behind her, in the first booth, a young couple sat with their heads face down on the table. Both had long kitchen knives sticking out of the backs of their necks. What looked like chili had been poured over their heads. The brown, meaty, bean-filled goo hid their faces from view.

At the counter, which had bar-style seating, an old man sat hunched over. He was face down in a giant bowl of what appeared to be chicken noodle soup. The yellowish substance was riddled with chunks of orange carrots and pieces of yellow corn as it curdled around his collar.

Next to him, an old woman sat, leaned against the counter. A server with bright orange hair and pale skin stood on the other side. She'd cut open the top portion of the old lady's head, had scooped out her brains, and was now ladling chicken noodle soup into her skull.

My legs trembled and warm piss soaked the front of my jeans and trickled down the insides of my legs. Vomit rose to the top of my throat and threatened to spew forth, but I swallowed it down. This was the vilest, most disgusting thing I had ever seen.

The naked Asian woman squatting only a few feet from me glanced my way and grinned. "Do you have splatterpunk?" she asked.

I couldn't respond. This couldn't be real.

The woman behind the counter, scooping soup into the old lady's skull repeated the question with, "Yeah, do you have splatterpunk?"

Before I had the chance to answer, the window behind me shattered, and Holbrook Johns's giant arm reached through and grabbed me around my throat as he shouted, "Do you have splatterpunk?!"

I jerked awake from the simulation and nearly flipped out of my seat. Tabitha, Doctor Shaw's assistant, raced into the room quickly and detached the electrodes connected to my forehead and temples. She must have known if she didn't, I would yank back and forth and possibly damage them.

"That was quite the trip," Tabitha said.

"Why did you leave me in so long?" I asked, pulling at the metal shackles keeping my wrists locked in place. They were meant to make sure I wouldn't fall off the chair.

At least that's what they'd told me. Now, I was feeling like they were meant to keep me in place, secure, locked-up.

"Dr. Shaw wanted to see how far you would go," she replied.

"Think you can unlock me?"

"Let's wait and see what the doctor says. He might want to put you back under."

"No, I don't want another dive. Not there. I almost died in there."

"It's not real," she reminded me. "It's only a simulation."

"It feels pretty real. The pain. It really hurts. Have you been in there?"

"No," she said with a shake of her head. I sensed a bit of sympathy as she added, "I haven't."

Glancing around the room, I took notice of its coldness. Grey, concrete walls, a TV screen mounted on one wall, and a counter with some tools on it. Other than that, there was only a rolling cart with a few monitors and some other equipment.

Dr. Shaw entered the room, in the white scrubs he typically wore. While Tabitha dressed down, usually in jeans and a T-shirt, he always looked ready to jump right into surgery.

"Thanks for your help, Tabitha," the doctor said. "Go ahead and check on our other subjects, please."

She smiled at me and left the room.

Dr. Shaw checked a readout on one of the computers as he spoke to me. "So, that was an interesting dive."

"If by interesting you mean I almost got hacked to pieces, then yeah, it was pretty interesting."

The doctor chuckled.

"Can you unlock me?" I asked.

"In a second."

Why is he hesitating to unlock me? Just unlock me already.

"There's one thing that really bothers me about your dive."

"What is it, Doc?"

"That you think splatterpunk is the mindless, pointless killing of people. Just gore for gore's sake. You know, my brother writes splatterpunk."

"Huh?"

"Yeah, and in your dive. All that killing you experienced, you associated it with splatterpunk… all that gore without any real point to it."

The doctor reached for a TV remote control that was sitting on the counter and turned on the wall-mounted TV. The screen flickered to life and the doctor changed the channel until it settled on the news where there was live footage of cops surrounding a building. The reporter, Rex Alvarez, was mid-explanation.

"… and the Shaw Center for Neurologic Stimulation is not responding but police have the building surrounded."

Wait. This is Dr. Shaw. Isn't this that center? Is this THAT *Dr. Shaw?*

"Where we've heard," Rex Alvarez continued, "Dr. Armin Shaw and his associates have taken the children of members of Congress hostage until they can reach a decision that tightens our nation's border security. You may recall that Dr. Shaw's wife was murdered last year when two illegal immigrants violently—"

Dr. Shaw turned off the TV. He approached me and stuck the electrodes to my forehead and temples.

"Wait, you said you were going to pay me to—" I started.

"Don't be a fool," the doctor interrupted. "Only pain is the payment. It was easier to get you here if you were willing rather than forced."

"You tricked me?"

"I'm afraid it was necessary, son."

"I don't understand the point," I said.

"You didn't hear the news? You and the other children were taken to convince your parents, the democrats and republicans, to finally work together to do the right thing. To do *some*thing. To do *any*thing that will put in place a process to allow good immigrants like my family to enter this country and filter out all the evil that doesn't belong here."

"But the dives. Why are you hurting us?"

"You're a twenty-two-year-old man," he replied. "Figure it out. I have a ten-year-old in the other room who's smarter than you."

"Please," I begged. "Don't make me dive again."

"That ten-year-old is afraid of sharks, so guess what his dive involves? Two rooms over is a fifteen-year-old girl who's afraid of heights. We've made her fall from the Eiffel Tower, tossed her out of an airplane... she's suffering. You? You don't seem to be afraid of much except serial killers. But what's interesting is you rather enjoy horror stories. You like splatterpunk but don't really understand there's a lesson to the story. A moral. Like punk rock music. Thumbing your nose at the man."

"Please," I begged. "I get it. I really do. Just let me go."

"It's pretty ironic, isn't it?" Dr. Shaw continued. "Quite fitting actually. There's a lesson here, to this story. You're suffering because your rich, shit-eating father is secure in his home while our families are getting raped and murdered by illegal felons. And until he figures out a solution, his son will pay for it. This here is the lesson..." he held up a finger and rolled it around as if pointing at all the walls in the room. "Now, enjoy your splatterpunk and all the killing and gore that goes along with it."

Dr. Shaw pressed a button.

I heard a loud *beep.*

Then the crash of glass.

A hairy arm reached around my throat.

In front of me, the naked Asian woman stood from where she'd been crouched on the floor. She held the ladle in her hand. Her wild eyes and bloody grin were fixed on me.

From behind, Holbrook Johns said, "Do you have splatterpunk?"

Both demented, murderous women in The Soup(er) Bowl asked, "Do you have splatterpunk?"

"Do you have splatterpunk?"

It should have been such a simple question.

I was plunged into the horror that night. Thrown right in like a kid who can't swim tossed into a lake by a deadbeat dad who wants to prove his machismo by making the boy kick to the surface with death nipping at his heels. Let me back up a bit.

Leave
Kristopher Rufty

I hate the summer. Too many bugs. The windshield was splattered with insects from driving these mountain roads. Didn't matter how many times Walker used the windshield cleaner. The wipers only smeared the bug guts into a cloud that darkened the windshield.

And it was damn hot. Even with the a/c cranked high, I was still sweating in my T-shirt and jeans. Probably because four of us were packed inside the tiny SUV, adding more muggy air than the car could keep up with.

"It's pretty out here," said Kevin from the backseat. "Lots of trees. Looks like the Sherwood Forest or something."

I snorted. "Take a picture while you can. Dad's tearing it all down soon as he owns it."

"That's a bummer."

"It is what it is."

Walker slowed almost to a stop at a sharp curve to avoid soaring off the edge of the mountain. My baby brother had never cared much for heights but always insisted on driving because he got carsick as a passenger.

The car moved around a protruding wall of rock that almost touched the road. The trees covering the ridge threw down heavy shade that made it look like night.

None of us had talked a whole lot. We rarely did when Dad sent us out on these adventures. Only Walker and I were related. Kevin and Jason were just friends from our childhood we'd hired to help with the grunt work.

Just show her I mean business, Dad had said from behind the desk in his nice office. The office with the heavy-duty air conditioner. This close to August in North Carolina was like driving with the sun as a passenger.

Maybe it was the job causing the sweats and silence this time. Something about this one had rubbed the boys the wrong way.

Jason, seated directly behind me, had been the quietest of all. "What's bothering you, Jason?"

He sighed. "Not really looking forward to intimidating an old lady, Donnie."

I could relate to his mood. "I don't relish the idea of it."

"But here we are."

"Yeah," I said. "Why wouldn't we be? It's like any other job Dad would send us on."

Walker adjusted himself behind the wheel, holding it with one hand now. That made me nervous because we weren't away from the dangerous curves yet. "What are we going to do?"

I shrugged. "Nothing any different then we usually do."

Walker winced. "I'm not beating up an old woman."

"We will if we have to."

Kevin and Jason both made sounds of disagreement in the back seat. I turned, putting my back against the passenger door to see everyone. The seatbelt rubbed my neck. "Her age doesn't change what we do if we *have* to do it."

"She's an old lady," said Jason. "Your dad said she was in her eighties."

"*And?*"

"My grandmother is in her eighties. She bakes pies and cookies and shit. What if we get there, and she's just taken a pan of fresh-baked chocolate chip cookies from the oven."

Kevin moaned. "I haven't had fresh-baked cookies since I was a kid."

I almost smacked him. "If my dad offered your grandmother several million dollars for her property, she'd probably sell it. She could make cookies and shit in a much nicer house in a fancier oven. One of those with the digital displays."

"There's nothing wrong with my grandmother's house. And she'd never understand how the digital stuff works."

"That's not what I'm saying."

"I get it. But old people are attached to things."

"This old lady's *attached* to eight hundred acres of overgrown land?" I asked. "She probably hasn't even seen all of it. How could she want to keep that much for herself?"

"She probably has family she wants to leave it to."

"Family would rather have the money, I'm sure."

Jason shook his head, looked out the window.

We drove even deeper into the mountains until finally finding a busted path that was nearly concealed with overgrown trees, marked by a rusted mailbox acned with tarnish-ringed holes.

"That's it," I said, pointing.

"I see it," said Walker. Slowing the SUV, he steered onto the gravel. The car bounced as the tires left the blacktop.

"Use the four-wheel-drive," I said.

Nodding, Walker pulled the lever, engaging the tires. It did nothing to smooth out the ride, but it made it manageable.

Tree limbs drooped onto our path like loose hairs, rubbing against the doors with sharp squeaking sounds.

"Are you sure this is even a driveway?" asked Kevin.

Walker shrugged, then bounced when the tires dropped into a hole. "Maybe at one time it was."

The ride was long and bumpy, but we finally reached a spot where the trees spread out around a weed-choked yard. Sitting in the centre of the tall grass was a ramshackle two-story house with dark windows coated in dust. What paint remained on the shoddy structure had turned grey and flaky, peeling away like dead skin.

An ancient truck sat at an angle in front of the slanting front porch. I could tell the tires were bald and dry-rotted even from where I sat in the car. Maybe at one time it had been green, but now it was a rusted brown with little islands of a mossy hue spread here and there.

"Somebody *lives* here?" said Jason.

"Yeah," I said. "Your grandma."

"Up yours, Donnie."

"Wouldn't you take a multimillion-dollar payout if you lived like this?"

"*I* would, yeah," said Jason. "Doesn't mean *she's* going to." Jason pointed toward the house.

I followed the path of his finger and saw the old woman had already come out onto the porch. A huge gash split the screen of the storm door behind her, killing its main purpose for existing.

At first glance, the old hag could've been mistaken for a skeletal Halloween prop, wearing an old, faded dress. Her hair was long and messy, the color of spiderwebs. Her skin was not unlike the underbelly of a fish, a dull color that made her look like a corpse.

"Jesus," said Walker, bringing the SUV to a stop. "She's prehistoric."

"So is everything else around here," I said, opening my door.

Walker shook his head, killed the engine.

The four of us climbed out. The collective thumps of our doors shutting echoed against the barriers of trees all around us.

The old woman seemed unphased, watching us with an almost amused curiosity. Like she'd never seen people like us in all her life.

God, I'd never seen such an old thing in real life.

"Who the fuck are you?" she said, her voice shrill and southern. "And what the fuck do you want?"

As always, the guys waited for me to speak. Somehow, I'd become the spokesperson for these meetings.

I walked toward the porch, the guys hanging close behind me. I'd almost reached the steps when she held up a haggard hand.

"That's far enough, mister." Her chin moved as if she were gnawing on something. But I figured that was impossible since she didn't seem to have any teeth. Her face was pruned and dark, sunbaked like old leather.

"Fine," I said. "I assume you can hear me okay?"

"My hearing's fine, smartass."

I smiled. "We represent Lamont Wilson."

"Ah," she said. "The great Larry Wilson. The country boy-turned-tycoon."

I hadn't heard Dad referred like that before. "Tycoon?"

"Bigshot."

"Oh. Right. Yeah. He does see himself as that." I put on a pleasant face for her. The same one I use whenever I want a girl at the bar to trust me into taking her home. "We understand he made you an offer on all your land."

The woman spat. A thick wad hit the dirt at my feet. She probably expected me to jump back, or grimace. I didn't even flinch. She didn't get to do the intimidation. That was *my* job.

"He's actually made you a few offers," I added. "And he sent us to offer you two more. Well, one offer and a choice."

"I can't hardly wait to hear it."

"Four million. A million more from the last offer."

"And the choice?" The old hag tilted her head. A breeze made her stringy hair flutter.

"Your choice is either taking the offer, or we'll have to…" I held out my arms, then used a hand to lift my shirt enough she could see the gun tucked in my pants.

"Shoot me?" the woman asked. "Seems rather extreme. Don't you boys think?" She looked at Jason. "Don't you think so?"

"Don't talk to him," I said. "Talk to me. You and I are having the conversation."

"Is we?"

I nodded. "I don't think you're taking me seriously."

The woman snorted. "A boy still wet behind his ears like you don't get my attention much. Do you know who I am?"

"Delilah Jenkins," I said.

"Smart feller. But do you know who I *was?*"

"Couldn't care less."

"I terrorized this sorry state of North Carolina for years. Before even yer daddy were a pearl drop in yer grandpap's nutsack."

"Spoken like a true hick," I said.

"I was never a hick, son. I just chose this place to be my home."

"Hick."

Delilah's top lip trembled.

"Jenkins," said Walker. Delilah turned to him, her gapped mouth splitting her face into a smile. "Ma Jenkins?"

She laughed a husky laugh and clapped. "Damn right, boy! Glad to see somebody knows their history."

"Who the fuck is that?" I asked, then wanted to kick myself. I couldn't let her think I cared at all. Not that I did, really, but I had to admit I was a little intrigued to know how Walker heard of her.

"She's famous," said Walker, looking at all of us. "Robbed banks, killed people."

167

"Stopped counting deaths at thirty-three," she said with a shrug. "Just became a normal thing to me, popping off a life here and there. Always tried to pick somebody I felt deserved it. But when they gunned down my family in fifty-seven, I went a little crazy. Started killing everybody. Didn't give a damn who it was. Blowed up some police stations, too. Killed feds." She sighed. "Got carried away with it for a while. But a girl had to retire."

I stared at this haggard woman who'd looked on the verge of turning to dust when we'd arrived. Now, some of the age seemed to have ticked away. I saw a wild youthfulness in her eyes that somehow shaved off several years.

And it scared me.

Right then was when I should have apologized to her, taken the boys, and left. But my damn pride, my stubbornness, and the fear of facing Dad when we got back kept me there.

I removed my gun, holding it out. I clicked off the safety.

"Are you going to take the money?"

Delilah shrugged. "Don't need it. I've got plenty buried all around here. I'm pretty sure that's why yer daddy wants my property. He'd probably come out with a high profit from my money and what he'd make selling it. But I never liked the Wilson family. Yer grandpap was the federal marshall that slaughtered my family. So, I ain't got no pleasure ever doing business with the likes of a Wilson."

I hadn't heard any of that information before. I wondered if Dad had known prior to sending us out here.

Of course he had, I realized. It was probably his plan all along.

I sighed. A part of me was impressed by her audacity. Another part was fed up with her. "Fine," I said. My finger tightened around the trigger, preparing to squeeze. "I guess we're done talking."

"Lemme say something," she said. "Since your daddy's too yellow-striped to come out here hisself, I'll give you the same choice ye gave me since you didn't know what you's walking into. Leave now. Don't come back. Or stay and die." She held out her hands, raising her shoulders. "Blunt, I know. But I'm old, so I'm allowed to be."

I laughed. It wasn't the reaction I'd expected to give her, but it just jumped out of me. I shook my head. "I'd like to say I'm not going to take any pleasure in killing you. But we both know that's a lie."

Delilah smirked. "Ah, well. Can't say I didn't try to be civil."

Before I even realized what was happening, Delilah had moved her arm to her skirt, flipped it back, and snatched a revolver from a holster strapped to her boney thigh. I glimpsed pale skin, lined with purple veins before the skirt fluttered back down.

I saw her raising her gun, so I pulled the trigger of mine. There was a boom. Something pounded my hand, throwing it back just as my gun went off. The shot went high as the gun flew out of my grip.

Her shot tore through my hand, spinning me around. Yelling, I pulled my injured hand to my chest, wrapping it in my shirt as blood flowed from the dark circles her bullet made on both sides.

"Shit!" Jason managed to shout as he went for his own gun. He jerked it loose from the hidden holster right before another shot blew off part of his head. I watched a massive chunk fly away, taking his left eye and part of his cheek with it.

Then Walker's hands were on me, dragging me toward the SUV while more shots rang out.

Bullets whistled past me, smacking the side of the SUV. The passenger window shattered in a spray of glass.

"Fuck!" Kevin cried out. I briefly wondered if he'd been hit, but I saw him dashing around the back of the SUV.

Bullets slapped the ground at his feet, throwing up plumes of dust.

Then I heard the click of her revolver hitting an empty round.

"Now!" I yelled. "Light her up!"

I turned around, pulling away from Walker as he stepped forward, lifting his .45, already firing.

The old hag was no longer standing there. Bullets from Walker and Kevin punched into the old wood, splitting it apart.

"Stop!" I yelled over the gunfire.

They halted their firing. Gunsmoke hung in the air like a fog reeking of old eggs.

"Did we get her?" asked Kevin.

I shrugged. "Who cares? Let's get out of here. My hand is fucked."

The blood had soaked through my shirt, mixing with the sweat on my stomach. The pain was incredible, but not nearly as bad as I figured it would be.

Walker opened the passenger door. "Shit. There's glass all over the place."

"I don't give a shit." I rushed over to the door.

"Going so soon?" Delilah's voice sounded like a cackling witch, shrill and looney.

We turned around just as she rose from behind the porch barrier, clutching something large in both hands. It had a barrel on top, extending from a round base below it.

"Fuck!" Kevin managed to yell before his body began jerking as rounds from her tommy gun ripped through him. Blood shot out his back in a series of red blossoms.

Walker fired back, but his shots were pointless. She'd already ducked back down. The screen door took the hits, cracking in half, hanging on by the old hinges in pieces.

Walker grabbed my arm and flung me into the SUV. My ass dropped onto the shards all over the seat. I was jabbed and poked several times.

Walker ran around the front of the car, jumped into his seat, and cranked the car in one motion.

He pulled the gear and stomped on the gas, taking off before either of us had shut the door. The wind rushing at us took care of it for us.

"Fuck," he said, looking in the rearview mirror. "I hate to leave them like that."

"Nothing else we could do," I said. I tore off the bottom part of my shirt, wrapping it around my hand like a bandage. "Fucking Dad knew she was like this."

"He couldn't have."

I didn't agree with that. "He knew more than he let on."

"What's the plan?"

"Get to civilization. Call Dad. Get my hand fixed."

Walker nodded. He glanced at the rearview mirror. "You've gotta be fucking kidding me!"

I turned around and gazed out through the back windshield. Dust swirled and shivered behind us, spreading around the rusted grille of the old truck that had been parked at the house. The old clunker was gaining on us fast, its engine roaring like a plane falling out of the sky.

I watched as a section on each side of the truck flew off. At first, I thought the piece of shit was falling apart. But when an additional modification began to reveal itself from the openings, I realized we couldn't be so lucky.

What I was seeing couldn't be real. And yet it was very real.

"Give me your gun," I said.

"You're hand!"

"I'll shoot with the other! Now!"

Walker handed it over. It felt weird because it was the wrong gun in the wrong hand. But it would have to do.

Because the Gatling guns that had emerged from the sides of the truck would tear us apart within seconds.

The sphere of barrels was pointing directly at us.

I started firing. The bullets seemed to be going everywhere except for the truck. I could see Delilah's craggy face above the steering wheel, her shoulders hunched up as her toothless grin made the lower half of her face look like a dark chasm.

Then the Gatling's barrels started spinning. She must have been operating the guns somehow from the inside, maybe a modified contraption she'd designed. This old lady was scary smart. And deadly.

A second later the barrels began spitting fire. The back of the SUV exploded open as thick bolts of lead tore through.

I heard Walker scream and turned to watch the front of my brother blow apart, showering the steering wheel with his blood and innards. His body was unable to halt the speed of the rounds. They smashed into the instrument panel, showering the cab with sparks.

Then we were veering hard to the left. the front end of the SUV tearing into the brush. Vines and leafy branches covered the windshield like the thick ribbons of a carwash. They slid away and I saw nothing but open air. The front of the SUV tipped down.

Then I saw the rushing water coming to meet me fast.

Closing my eyes, I waited for death to come get me as well.

When I opened my eyes again, I was in a hospital bed. My body was rigid inside the full cast that made me look twenty pounds heavier. Both legs were connected to cables that suspended them above the foot of the bed. The only piece of me that didn't seem to be held together by plaster was my face.

From the way my vision looked, I knew I was only seeing through one eye. Whether that was permanent or not, I had no idea.

Dad was sitting beside the bed in a chair that looked as if he'd had it delivered there. There was way too much padding for it to have been provided by the staff.

Seeing I was awake, he closed the Bible he'd been reading from. "Thank God," he said. "I was starting to think you weren't ever waking up."

He wore a suit, as always. His grey hair was slicked straight back, held there with a surplus amount of gel.

I tried to speak, but my throat felt like it had been scrubbed with sandpaper. He called the nurse for me and got me some ice water. It was like liquid Heaven when I drank it.

Dad gave me a few more minutes to come around before he started in with the questions.

I told him everything, then brought up the fact that she seemed to think he'd known who she was.

"Yeah," he said. "I knew."

"And you sent us anyway? Sent us against somebody like her. Unprepared!"

"How was I supposed to know that would happen? She's in her nineties. She should barely be able to walk."

"She could do *a lot* more than walk!"

Dad took a deep breath, let it out slowly. "I sent another team out there. Bigger, armed better."

"Educated better than your own sons, I hope."

I could tell that remark stung. His lips tightened into a thin line. "I'm sorry, son. I didn't want that to happen to you or your brother. But he'll be avenged. I made sure of it. They're supposed to bring me her head."

I stared at Dad, unable to comprehend the kind of person he was. I knew somewhere deep down, he truly felt sorry for what had happened. He'd never say it, though. He'd never admit Walker was killed because of his greed, either.

But it was no longer my problem. He'd handled it. Like he always did.

The team Dad sent out there to avenge us never came back.

Neither did the second, larger team.

Or the third.

Friday Night in Damascus
Brian Keene

The world generally agrees on Friday night.

Regardless of culture or social and religious mores, Friday night is when things happen. Elton John once suggested that Saturday night is alright for fighting, and that may be so, but Friday night is for fun.

In the great cities all across the world, people go to nightclubs and bars on Friday night. They dance and drink and flirt and fuck. There is laughter and shouting and music, and if there are screams, they are usually screams of joy. There are sporting events—high school football, soccer matches, and countless more. There are art gallery showings to attend, movie theaters and concert halls, plays and stand-up comedy. People go to book signings and poetry readings and religious services and group therapy sessions. They attend parties for birthdays and anniversaries and job promotions and just because. Friday night is also for the housebound and the introverted and the socially awkward. They stay at home, put on comfy clothes and cuddle up with a partner or a child or a beloved pet. They Netflix and chill. They play video games and board games and card games together. They read or talk or sit in sedate silence, enjoying the company of another or basking in their solitude.

Friday night occurs at different times across the globe, but all of these things are occurring on Friday night.

They are happening in New York City. Beijing. Los Angeles. Lagos. Mumbai. Chicago. Karachi. Tokyo. Moscow. Cairo. London. Seoul. Philadelphia. Bangkok.

But Friday nights in Damascus are different. Oh, maybe not at first glance. The city seems to have a vibrant nightlife. And you might think that two-story stone building sitting at the end of an industrial block in the southern part of the city is nothing more than a goth nightclub. The assumption is easy to make, given the architecture and dim lighting and dirty dungeon decor. But it's not throbbing bass or muffled cries of ecstasy you hear when standing outside the building on a Friday night.

No. It's the wails and the shrieks of the damned.

That dungeon decor isn't just decor. It's an actual dungeon, and it's only one of many spanning the country. They are housed in converted factories and hospitals and concert halls and places of worship, and on Friday nights, they host a different sort of revelry.

There is an old man in Lewisburg, West Virginia. On Friday night, he attends the local high school football game. He sits in the bleachers, sipping a hot chocolate and cheering. There is an old man in Damascus. On Friday night, he is stripped naked and beaten with an iron rod until he faints. To wake him up again, his captors douse him in scalding hot chocolate and then cheer as he screams.

There is teenager in Toronto, Canada. On Friday night she goes skinny-dipping with her friends. She shivers with excitement. There is a teenager in Damascus. On Friday night, she is drowned repeatedly in a tank of sewage water, until ultimately, her captors are unable to revive her. They then hose her off and take turns having sex with her corpse.

There is a marching band in Boise, Idaho. On Friday night, the drum major leads them, twirling a baton. There is a marching band in Damascus. On Friday night, a torturer presses an electric baton to each of their genitals, shocking them one by one.

There is a man in Northampton, United Kingdom. On Friday night, he sits in his recliner, absentmindedly stroking his beard while reading a good book. There is a man in Damascus. On Friday night, he is strapped to a metal chair. An electric current is then passed through it until his beard begins to curl and smoke. He bites down so hard that his teeth shatter, becoming jagged knives that slash his tongue and cheeks.

There is a group of children in the Netherlands. On Friday night, they sit around a campfire, toasting marshmallows and telling stories. There is a group of children in Damascus. On Friday night, all of them are tortured with fire. The methods vary per child. Oil, chemicals, gasoline, and even gunpowder are used. One has insecticide sprayed all over his small body. Then he is set alight. He flees, shrieking, before slamming into a wall. His torturers wrap him in gauze bandages but offer no other medical care. In the days that follow, the boy lays twitching with shock and infection while his jailers lift up sections of bandage and slice away portions of his burned flesh. These charred morsels are then force fed to other children.

In Mexico City, a group of twenty-somethings spend Friday night just hanging out together. In Damascus, another group of twenty-somethings do the same thing. But their Friday night involves hanging suspended by their wrists, dangling and spinning until their shoulders are dislocated.

On Friday night in Kentucky, a group of men gather at a garage, listening to the radio, drinking beer, and changing the tires on a car. On Friday night in Damascus, a man is stuffed inside a car tire. His bones are broken until he fits securely. He is then beaten and rolled around, and then flung off a building to see if he'll bounce. His spine gives way long before the tire treads do.

A young couple in Paris recently moved in together, and they spend their Friday night putting down new carpet in their apartment. A young couple in Damascus spends their Friday night on the "Flying Carpet"—a device consisting of a long wooden board, hinged so that it folds in the middle. They are strapped to this and then bent. While they can still scream, they beg for crucifixion, for a bullet, for anything other than this. Their captors laugh, and then redouble their efforts until the victim is bent in half.

On Friday night in Damascus, eyes are gouged, tongues are torn out, and fingernails are pulled. Heads get crushed, teeth get smashed, organs are removed, and appendages—everything from fingers and toes to penises and clitorises—get snipped off. Lips are stapled shut, noses are blocked with glue, and ears have nails driven into them.

When Friday night is over, and the sun rises over the great cities all across the world, people go about their daily lives, and get on with their Saturday.

But in Damascus, it is always Friday night.

Story Notes

The obscene brutality and various tortures mentioned in this story are all based on documented cases from Syria, where over two hundred thousand people are detained and tortured at any given time. The Syrian Network for Human Rights, a global non-profit organization, documents that between March 2011 and September 2019, nearly fifteen thousand—including one hundred and seventy-eight children and sixty-three women—died in Syria as a result of torture and horrific abuse. More than fourteen thousand victims died at the hands of Syrian government's torturers, while Islamic extremist groups killed fifty-seven through torture. Factions of the armed opposition tortured and killed a further forty-three, while forty-seven people were tortured and killed under the control of the Syrian Democratic Forces (SDF), and another twenty were tortured and killed by parties the group was unable to identify.

About the Editor

Jack Bantry is the editor of Splatterpunk Zine. He also co-edited Splatterpunk Fighting Back and Splatterpunk Forever (along with Kit Power), both winners of the Splatterpunk-award for Best Anthology. He resides in a small town at the edge of the North York Moors.

Printed in Great Britain
by Amazon